RED DEAD JANE

Freedom's Charge

by

D.P. Pankratz

Copyright

Red Dead Jane is a complete work of fiction, other than names of Kings, (Philip IV, and James I), ships names, (Prince Royal and certain places that are real. Any other names, places, or persons living or dead is completely coincidental.

Published in the United States by Lulu.com

LIBRARY AND ARCHEIVES CANADA CATALOGING-IN-PUBLICATION DATA

Pankratz, Perry (Perry P.)

Red Dead Jane/D.P. Pankratz

Red Dead Jane: Freedoms Charge /D.P. Pankratz

ISBN 978-1-9992417-4-2

Printed in the United States of America

Lulu.com

First Edition

Red

Red

A Fire burns

On the coldest night of summer, I looked up towards the heavens for any sign of how I didn't see this coming months before the fateful delivery. I was driven to the furthest parts of civilization by King James I of England and King Philip IV of Spain. I was separated from my loved ones for over a year and a half because of that damned piece of paper. Declared a traitor by both Kings for inciting war, I barely eluded England's grasp with my head attached to my shoulders.

Glancing around with tear-filled eyes, I hope to catch a glimpse of anything that resembles home. Or, at least something not trying to kill me or my men. I've had to do things—things I'm sure would have my father's stomach churning. England and Spain sent many a ship after us in hopes of hanging my lifeless body from the gallows of their lavish flagships. No matter what happens, I will prove my innocence and show everyone their true colors. I'll continue slaughtering their men and sinking their ships to the depths of hell.

Turning towards a noise, off from our bow, I see what seems to be the outline of a ship in the distance, her stern facing towards us. Both ships teeter from side to side in the waves. I listen closely for any yelling coming from the ship, but only the sea makes any sound.

Red

Everyone aboard our ship, the Lady of the Damned, quickly and quietly readies the cannons on both sides. The sound of sloshing water hits the bow hard, as we start coming around their rear.

"Unknown ship! Man the stations!" I hear a Spanish man yell.

An evil smile comes over my face as I shout, "Fire!" Our cannon balls dissect their ship, splintering her mid and upper hull into hundreds of pieces. Their screams howl like wounded dogs in my ears. They scramble like rats avoiding the light, trying to inch their cannons towards the lady of the Damned. Their guns coming into range and begin firing as do ours. I drop onto the deck as wood splitters fly all around me. Looking up, I see a Spanish soldier jump onto our deck. He makes a run for me, but I pull my pistol up and fire.

"I almost killed you, Red…" he whispers, as he falls inches in front of me.

I grin as my eyes focus on him, "almost doesn't cut it!" Pulling out my sword, I thrust it into his neck. Listening to the cannons being reloaded, we turn our bow and head towards her stern again.

"Fire!" Their captain yells.

The ship fires back at us once again, but half of cannon balls splash into the water. A hard right and our guns fire at her gun ports. All but three of the gun ports are working on her left side.

"Stay on this side of her," I shout, grinning. Swinging the ship to the left, we find ourselves coming alongside her wounded side. Dozens of men are waiting for us on their barely lit deck. Waiting for us to get close enough to jump aboard and attack. As we get closer, we unload another round of cannon fire, sending some of their men flying across the deck and clearing a path for us to come aboard. Antwon turns the Lady into the Spanish ship, scraping against the hull.

Everyone looks at me as I shout, "Get the dogs!"

My men shout and jump aboard their ship before they have a chance to regroup from the blast. The clinking of swords mixes with the screams of the dying and wounded. We fight with our hearts and souls attached to our weapons, decimating their numbers one slash at a time. I know the Captain must be nearby as they run to protect a doorway with their lives. Within minutes of engaging the Spanish soldiers, the last in front of the door falls.

The door begins to open slowly as we wait for more scurvy dogs to come charging at us. Surprise comes over me when the Captain comes out, his sword laid upon both palms waiting for me to take it. Walking over the dead bodies lying on the deck, I slip on blood as I get closer to the Captain. He kneels, his eyes filled with hate, as he states solemnly, "I relinquish my command, but know King Philip will put your neck in a noose for this traitorous act against one of his ships."

Grabbing the sword from his palms, I raise the sword high above my head. "I have no intentions of hanging. Not until I clear my name," I answer, angrily, lowering the Captain's sword close to his throat. Thrusting the sword high again, my men shout cheerfully.

Red

I look down at the captain who is glaring up at me with a hatred I've seen before.

"What is your name, wench?" he asks.

"Red Dead Jane!" I exclaim, smiling as my eyes lock onto him.

He straightens his collar as he proclaims, "King Philip will know your name, Red. When your time comes, you will hang from the highest yardarm. Your days are numbered."

I adjust the position of the sword so the blade presses against his throat, and see the fear grow in his eyes.

"Your king already knows my name. He along with the King of England already want me dead. Their plan was to bring two nations together using my skin as their bond, but I will keep my skin."

"You are but a woman. You will not keep your head long…"

I press his sword even harder against his throat, cutting him off as the sword pierces his throat slightly. "I intend to keep my head. Beware the next words out of your mouth, Captain. Or you might find your sword piercing your heart in two," I reply, reminding him where his sword is.

"Okay, calm down. We will not resist you any longer."

"You are right, Captain, you won't put up a fight any longer. I have special plans for you and your men come dawn. I swore to your king I would destroy his and King James' fleets, leaving their shores baron of any ships to stop invasions. As soon as the sun rises up, you will choose your death, Captain."

"You cannot do that. You are the devil herself if you command such an order."

"Yes Captain, I am Spain and England's nightmare created by both them. You are a mere means to an end and as you can see, the sun is beginning to rise just beneath the horizon. Dear Captain, I must thank you for your hospitality. Choose. You can swim for the nearest shore, or you can burn with your ship. What will it be?" I ask, removing the sword from his throat and placing it against my shoulder, listening for his reply? His eyes burn like the devil himself, as he yells.

"You are a mad woman. Sharks await us if we swim, or we burn like heretics. There is no choice here, just disgrace."

"Choose, Captain! There is no debate here…"

"Plunge your sword through my heart."

"That was not the choice given to you. Regal, tie our friends to the mast. Since the Captain will not choose, he shall burn with his ship."

Regal grabs the Captain and one of the soldiers and ushers them towards the mast. As they struggle to free themselves, my men ignite the passionate fire. We quickly disembark from their ship back to ours and slowly drift away, watching the flames dance seductively across the deck towards them. I see the fear in the Captain's eyes as the flames caress them; their screams of agony are short lived. We sail away and I watch their ashes float to the heavens while their bodies sink to hell. We celebrate our victory as the smoke becomes less and less.

"Well done, Red. Rack up another ship to their losses. Twenty-nine so far. You have made us rich. Hooray for our Captain!" Antwon says cheerfully.

"Thank you. We all play our parts in this victory, here is to you as well," I reply, raising the dead captain's sword above my head.

"Where to next, Captain?" Antwon asks.

"Death Island. We must make repairs to our girl before engaging them again. That last shot seemed pretty low," I reply, as a couple of men go check for what damage we took. Soon they rush back to my side.
"Yes, Captain, it was just that. Three feet above the water, may be a bit more."

"We will set sail for the cove," I answer, sternly. *"Those bastards will pay for this,"* I think.

"Aye, Aye Captain…making way to Death Island," Regal responds.

We sail for the next two days before coming to the island. We were almost sunk three times by waves trying to get into the belly of our ship. Landing in the cove of Death Island, the ship is crippled severely.

I took seven days of hellish work, night and day, to put the Damned Lady's hull back together. Once all the repairs were done, we celebrated with the finest ales Spain had to offer. After a full day of celebrating our victory over the Spanish, we readied our sails once more, this time for England's shores in search of another victory.

Twenty-seven days into our voyage and the seas have been kind to our Lady of the damned. We've had four more victories against one Spanish galleon and three English supply ships.

We start coming upon what seems to be a regular sailing ship. Grabbing the looking glass, I extend it to full length and stare. "Flying under the Denmark flag…what do you think Regal?" I ask, looking at the others.

"Let's get them, Captain. Let's show them who rules these seas," Regal yells.

"Very well, set sail for that ship!" I shout.

Slowly we catch up to the slower moving ship, but just before we're in firing range of her hull a white flag appears to be waving erratically near her stern.

"HOLD FIRE!" I yell, holding my hand up, pondering why they didn't raise the white flag sooner. We snug up against her hull and the wood makes a snapping sound. An old man stumbles to the rail with one hand raised in the air holding the flag and the other holding himself upright. He stares at us with a sickly expression.

Red

"Who are you, stranger?" he shouts, weakly.

"Red Dead Jane," I answer, proudly.

He almost falls down as a wave makes our ship tap his with some force. Barely catching his footing, he replies struggling to catch air, "I am Edger Townsend of Denmark. We surrender to your flag. We don't have much to plunder, but you are welcome to it. If only you let us be on our way, we have sailed for over half a year."

I glaring at him suspiciously, knowing this may be a trap. "Stand aside, we are boarding," I shout, as he stumbles backwards and I jump aboard, placing the tip of my sword close to his heart. I watch every movement he makes closely. Edward takes another step back, staring at my eyes, as my men begin boarding his ship.

"Where are your passengers?" I ask.

"They are all below. There are not many of us left. Death has visited us many times in a short while."

Walking to the door cautiously, Edward clumsily moves in front of me as we head below. I look around, appalled at the conditions and smell. There are mainly women and children aboard and they all look as if death is holding their hands, ready to walk them down that long path to the end. The stench of rotten flesh wafts throughout the galley. I collect only thirty silver pieces handed to me by Edger himself.

"There is nothing on this ship Red," Christian says, coming down the stairs. "Nothing worth plundering."

"I guess today is your lucky day, Edger. We will let you go in peace. Seems like you have already gained a curse from what I see here," I respond, looking around at their faces. Edger nods slightly.

"Yes, a curse indeed. From the English merchants. Their foods were our curse to bear: eat or die even though we were dead after eating. Many thanks for letting us travel on. Your kindness will shine among our people, if only for your actions here today."

"English swine. We shall force our swords down their throats for you," I reply, angrily.

"Thank you. Who are you again?"

"Red Dead Jane," I reply, confused. *"Perhaps the sickness is making him slow."*

"I hope we meet again so I can repay your kindness, Red Dead Jane," he says, placing his hands on mine.

"That may be a tough order to fill, Edger. My days are numbered as well. Maybe I will have the chance to stop by Denmark, and perhaps we will enjoy a drink together."

"That would be an honor, Red."

"Yes, we must go. We have to make the English pay for this and other deeds," I say, nodding.

Red

Jumping back aboard the Lady of the Damned, I look back at Edger knowing he will be long dead before he reaches his homeland. I wonder if it would not be easier to let the cannons roar on the starboard side. No, I cannot. Death already has them in his hands.

Antwon, throws over two sacks of canned food onto their deck. As we begin to drift apart, he raises his hand and waves.

"Let's head east," I tell Regal.

"Yes, Red."

A cold shiver grips my soul watching Edger's ship becoming smaller in the distance. I just can't help but wonder how close to home he'll get before falling for the last time.

Peek a boo

It's been another thirty-two days at sea and Edger still crosses my mind often. I wonder if he made it or succumbed to death's hands. Having just spotted a Spanish Galleon heading to the far side of an Island, we change our direction, planning to head them off on the other side. We will make this one a quick battle.

"The cannons are ready to fire. We are ready to slaughter them all, Red," Regal says, coming to stand by my side.

"Great, we'll give them a warm welcome," I answer, grinning.

Approaching the south side of the island, we begin to drift along the current. Hours pass with no sign of them so we start sailing, hoping to cut them off.

"Damn it. Did they head straight away from the Island? We will never catch up to them if they did," I shout, fighting back the anger.

Red

"We would have seen something if they had, Red. I'm sure of it," Regal responds.

Glancing around the waters, as the glare of the sun bounces off the water into my eyes.

"Maybe they saw us and made their way back to where they came from? We couldn't see if they turned back around," Dennis chimes in.

"That is a possibility," I nod. "They may have sailed that way and not have shown themselves while we were waiting. Let's make another trip around this Island. Maybe they needed to offload something. Perhaps we can catch them off-guard."

"Aye, Aye Captain, setting the sails high," Regal complies.

Watching carefully, we come to a cove in the Island, readying the cannons to fire. The cove opens up revealing nothing more than a small boat sitting ashore.

"Red, look atop the cliff there," Antwon says.

Looking up, I see a man signaling something on the other side of the Island.

"I see, so the Spanish want to play games? Let's make it even funnier. Watch that man's signals. Let's see if we can figure out where those scurvy dogs are hiding," I answer.

"He's signaling towards the other side of the island."

"I bet he knows we know he is there too. We'll keep on course. I am sure they are going to be headed this way, and we will fire upon them as if hell itself is right here. Wait for the signal."

"Yes, Captain. This will be another glorious victory for us," Regal says.

"Yes, it will… if I am right," I state, uncertain.

"Red, you have never not been right when it comes to these sea dogs."

"Perhaps they are learning from their mistakes. Everyone has to meet the devil eye-to-eye one day."

"Red, a ship is rounding the Island!" David shouts, interrupting us.

"All hands ready. Let's send them to hell!" I shout, looking to where David is pointing.

Before their main cannons come peeking through the rocks, our cannons lay waste to their bow. We can see men being thrown into the water. As our ship approaches the island's edge, we see the ship starting to lean towards the starboard side.

"Red… she should be sinking to her port side," Regal says, worried.

I nod, looking back up at the cliff. "That man on that cliff is still signaling. You do not think there are two ships, do you?"

Red

"I only saw one, Red…"

"Reload the cannons!" I yell. "I bet they knew we were coming, the dogs. If there is another ship, they will all burn, including that man on the cliff. Turn to our port side more, I bet they are coming up behind us."

"Port side!" I scream a few minutes later as another ship, an English Galleon, comes from where we had been hiding originally. Turning our bow towards them, we fire wildly, ducking as a piece of bow explodes.

"We were hit twice, not that bad," Regal shouts over the blows.

I stand back up and glare at the English, "Good. Turn starboard while they are reloading."

We start to turn and unleash our cannons one at a time, knocking their main mast off. They unleash their cannons again and we hit the deck as wood splinters fly everywhere.

"They hit one of our gun ports," someone shouts.

"Return fire!" I yell, pointing at the English.

Our cannons blast openly into the English ship. We sail straight at them as they unleash another round of fire at us. Once ready, we turn starboard again and unleash the ten cannons we have left. We see the white flag appear as the ship starts to burn. By the time we are close enough, the flames are dancing all over her deck. We leave the men in the water as we watch them be picked off by the large sharks.

Sighing, I look around at the mess on our deck and then back to watch the English galleon sinking slowly. Walking towards the stern, I grasp my spyglass and look at the English ship turning a bright orange in the setting sky.

Bottom's up

After two weeks resting on Death Island, we repair the Lady of the Damned as plans of more victories against the English and Spanish cross our lips. On the twelfth day of our stay, we gather around the table with our map spread out wide as we discuss the possible whereabouts of the English and Spanish ships. Everyone points to different positions on the map, waiting for my answer eagerly. My eyes fall towards a port of interest. I point at Hispaniola, "How about here? There are usually English, and sometimes Spanish, in this area. I remember when we were the king's messengers. They usually staked out the Island, waiting to catch pirates who came to enjoy themselves. Perhaps we should go enjoy ourselves?"

Antwon begins rolling up the map, "the ship will be prepared in a day, and ready to spill the blood of the English soon thereafter."

We spend the next two days loading the Lady with fresh supplies until we're finally ready to set sail for another round of revenge. Hoisting the anchor up, we drop the sails as the open waters take us to either the English or Spanish. Only time will tell what awaits us when we get there.

We finally anchor the Lady of the Damned just outside Hispaniola after seven days. Taking three rowboats in, we land on the shore at high noon. Walking toward the tavern, people stare, shocked to see me still alive. Heading inside the darkly lit tavern, I walk up to the barkeep.

"A round for everyone," I shout, flipping the barkeep a gold piece as the room erupts in cheers.

"Well then, I guess it is you the Spanish want. King Philip wants you hung on every one of his flagships. Has a thousand gold pieces weighing in on your head, Red."

"Did you hear that, boys? King Philip wants me on all his flagships."

"What makes a harlot like you so special?" a man in the corner yells through a thick English accent.

The laughter quickly stops, as everyone, including me, turns to the back corner. A well-dressed man with Dracula hair and beady little eyes is sitting alone. Grabbing my drink, I walk over to him.

"Who are you to ask such a question?" I ask, glaring at him as he sipped his ale, unbothered.

"Richard Hawkins. I am the 'sea dog'. So again, my question is: what makes a harlot like you so special?"

"I have taken out over thirty ships in as many months…both English and Spanish Galleons." I answer, smiling as his smug look fades.

"Yes, that is quite an accomplishment given that you're a mere messenger who betrayed the king himself. Maybe I should turn you over for the bounty."

"You will be lying dead in your drink before you could stand up to try," I answer, smiling.

"You are but a woman. You cannot stand up to the might of the Spanish Armada, or the great English Navy for that matter. Why not come to my bunk and I will protect you from those mean villainess men who seek to mess up that pretty face of yours."

"I will continue to stand against them. I would lay in a pile of thorn bushes naked before being with the likes of you. I don't need to be protected from men," I answer, disgusted.

"How dare you, you disrespectful…" he stutters, beginning to stand.

"Watch your tongue. Those next words may be your last," I say, holding my sword ready to pull and swing.

"One day we will meet in here or on the sea, and I will watch you drown in your own misery," he concedes, sitting back down. "I hope it's me who turns your bones over to the king."

I smirk, watching the hatred stew in his eyes. "Yes, I hope we meet upon the sea. I look forward to listening to your screams as you burn with your ship or are eaten by the sharks below. Sad to say there will not be a bone left to send to anyone. That will be your reward if you dare to tangle with me."

I wait for him to stand so I can plunge my sword into the deepest parts of his chest, but he just sits there, glaring back with his fists clinched. A young man walks up to us, stops and bows his head.

"Excuse me… Red Dead Jane? I am wondering if there is a place on your ship for another man," he says, still bowed.

"Who are you and why are you not on another ship?"

"John Welligham. Our ship was sunk off the coast of Easter Island by an American ship. I am hoping to find a ship that can be my home for longer than a month." His demeanor screamed English.

"I'm sorry to hear about your luck, but everyone knows our life expectancy is short," I answer.

"I know, but I have heard great things about the Lady of the Damned."

"As you should have. She is a good ship, but what makes you think you would be a good crew member?"

"I am well trained in the duties that are required," he says, standing up straight. "Swabbing the deck, cooking, and fighting…"

I eye him closer. "That is all good, but that is not what makes a good member of our crew. Our hearts bleed for our ship; each one of us willing to die for the other. You are better suited for a ship who is not involved in fighting. The Lady of the Damned expects you to bleed for her. You will find a ship, but it will not be on our ship," I answer, looking as his face angers.

"What kind of pirate does not accept another crew member knowing you have lost as many members in the last month as you…"

"The smart kind. You see, we all know where he Lady of the Damned gets her crew from, and it is not from this port. I guess the English have lowered the standards of assassins they send to kill me."

"I am not here to kill you…"

"Shut up! Your own mouth betrays your thoughts. I have a good mind to drag you behind our ship and let the sharks pick your bones clean. Go away before you feel the true steel of my vengeance."

I stand up, leaving him in confusion. Heading back to the rowboats, the men are already waiting for our return.

"We have taken one trip loaded with food and other necessities," Christen says, throwing a sack into the rowboat.

"Great. Once we get back to the ship, you and the others may come and have fun while we plan our next moves. A single cannon shot will let them know it is time to come back."

"I will let them know."

As we are rowing towards the Lady of the Damned, a shimmering light in the distance sends a bright reflective light our way.

"Look over there. What is that?" I ask.

"I do not know, Red. Looks like maybe light shining off a spyglass? Once we get on the ship, we should be able to get a better view," Regal responds.

We begin paddling faster to the ship, and climb aboard while the others load the supplies. Taking my spyglass out, the shining has disappeared, but I can see three pint-sized galleons coming towards us, flying under the English flag.

"All hands on deck! The English are coming," I yell, watching my crew load as quickly as they can. I run to the bow and begin bringing up the anchor. Just as I finish, I look at the ship in front of us, 'The Devon'. A row boat is approaching it, carrying Mr. Hawkins.

"Load three cannons on the port side and aim for just above the water line. Nail that ship in front of us," I say, turning to Adrian. *"Perhaps our friend Mr. Hawkins plans get us on our way out. We'll beat him to the punch."*

"I'm on it."

Heading back to the wheel, I begin turning to our starboard side. As more sails raised, we catch a good breeze and push faster. Then, one after another, the cannon fire smashes three holes just above the water line, guaranteeing Mr. Hawkins will not pursue us. His cannons fire back but miss as we are just out of reach. Using the spyglass again, I see the three ships still making their way towards us. As the wind catches our sails, we sail as if we weigh nothing, and soon the ships become nothing but a speck in the glass.

We continue to sail through the night and for the next three days. All is quiet while we check our maps.

"I believe we are at Mira por vas. If we continue our heading, we should run across Anguilla in another three or four days. We can resupply there and then we will have all the supplies we need to push into open waters for well over a month," I tell Regal.

"Yes, Red. We may meet some resistance at Anguilla if the Spanish still port there."

"We will look out for them, but if they stand up, we shall knock them down once again," I answer.

"Dinner is ready!" Samuel shouts.

Uproars of cheering begins as we settle in for dinner. Moving the maps aside, we sit as the waters churns and twists the boat making an ever so soft creaking sound.

"Ship starboard!" Christen yells, interrupting everyone.

We jump up and run onto the deck to see a shadow of a ship in the distance. I'm unable to see what flag she is running under.

"Ready the cannons," I say.

All we can do is watch as the last of the light fades. She is not flying a flag I can see, but then again, neither are we.

"Ahoy there," a man shouts cheerfully.

Looking at the shadow of a man standing on deck, an old friend's face emmerges before me. Jack Low; a friend going back to Ireland. He swings across onto our deck.

"It has been more than a few years since I have seen your eyes. I have missed you," he addresses me.

"Yes, it's been too long. What brings you around here?" I ask, curiously.

"Trading goods with the natives of Cuba. I hear there is a price on your head. Could it be because you sank all those ships?"

"No, they want me for treason. You see, they want to make peace between the two nations. They hired me to carry out messages for them. Well, they played each other, and I was caught in the middle. I never looked at the messages between the two of them. They believe I changed the messages and tried to cause the war to continue. So, now I am trying to clear my name," I answer.

"I see. They double-crossed each other and blame you. How long have you been running?"

Sighing, I look Jack in the eyes. "Over a year now. I hope I can clear my name, but that is unlikely as I cannot step on either's land without being hung."

"Yes, that is quite a dilemma. Dead if you do, dead if you do not. Would it help if we traded ships? Ours is equipped with heavier cannons; seven on each side."

"That is a generous offer, but we've had much luck with the Lady here." I answer.

"These guns are heavier than the Spanish or English cannons. These would give you an ultimate advantage against them."

"I appreciate the offer, but our Lady is quicker than any of their ships. We will be okay until our time comes."

"The offer will stand as long as we are here, in case you change your mind, Jane."

"Many thanks, but we will be fine until they finally catch up to us," I reply, patting him on the arm.

"You still are as brave as you are beautiful. I wish you luck on your journey and, a heads up, there are two English ships in that channel back the way we came."

"Thanks. We're not headed that way so we will miss them by miles." I answer, thinking,

"Well then, may your journeys bring you back home one day."

"Yes, one day I will be home. Hopefully alive and well. If I do not make it while I am in this world, tell my mother and father I love them both dearly," I answer as he stands on the ledge getting ready to swing back over to his ship.

"I will relay that message only if I hear you have perished at the hands of the kings," he answers, looking back at me.

He grabs the rope tighter, but one of his men shouts

"Sir! There's an English ship approaching our port!"

"Fire when they hit range!" Jack yells back, jumping down off the ledge.

"Turn to our port and support their fire," I shout.

The ship shifts and our guns are slowly turned to face the oncoming ship. The English ship is also turning to expose its guns. Jack's ship begins firing first, and the English return fire.

"Fire!" I scream when finally, we are ready. Our cannons lay rage upon their hull. Jack's ship returns another round. Only two of the English cannons return fire. Before long, we watch as the ship's crew raises a white flag.

"What do you want to do, Jane?" Jack asks, confused.

"Usually I would steal their gold and burn their ship," I answer, smiling.

"Okay, so do we head over then?"

"Yes, but maybe you should be on your ship so they do not claim you are pirates too. You can say they fired first. At least it will keep you from being known as a traitor to the crowns. I am already one," I answer.

He grabs my hand and kisses it before looking for the right moment to swing back over to his ship. He waves when he lands on deck. As we separate, we come up to each side of the English ship. The Captain takes one look my way, and I see the rage in his eyes. Before I can pull my pistol, he fires, hitting me in the shoulder.

Knocked down, my shoulder throbs in pain like someone was stabbing me and twisting the blade. I hear the cannon fire continuing. Out of the corner of my eye, I watch as the English ship slowly begins bottoming up. I hear the screams of men sent into the cold water and listen as the ship creaks and groans until the bottom is the only part above water.

"You tried and died for that shot, captain. Enjoy your rewards from the depths."

Red

Words of a Dead Pirate

Waking up on the shores of Death Island, my shoulders slung in such a fashion that I cannot move it. Dark menacing clouds roll in, signaling a storm coming on the horizon. I watch the water in the cove dancing. The white caps are small but noticeable.

"Curse that English dog. Once I am ready again, they will pay for each day I lay here," I think to myself.

Noticing me, Regal smiles and shouts excitedly.

"You're awake, Red. Hey, Red is awake! How are you feeling? We pulled the musket ball out and burned the skin closed. You'll probably be sore for a while."

Christen and the others join Regal until they're all standing in front of me, smiling.

"Yes, I cannot move it now, but I will feel it soon enough. I can't believe I didn't move before he shot," I state, anger filling my heart.

"Even I didn't see it until he had it out and firing," Regal responds. "I guess this means no one waving a white flag will get mercy from now on."

They look at me intently as they wait for my answer. I watch their eyes for any signs of mercy, but there are none.

"That is right. From now on, they will die with or without holding a white flag. They will burn for this," I reply, reaching for my shoulder.

"Death to them all!" the crew cheers.

After weeks of healing, spending hours getting my left shoulder mobile, finally I could swing my sword again.

The Lady of the Damned bobs around on the waves. The sun casts a shadow of her that seems to be reaching out towards me. I'm interrupted by the sound of shouting coming from some of the men on the ship. I turn to see them point out towards the sea.

"Red, there's a ship coming this way," Antwon says. "Do you want us to wait, or should we fire upon her as she comes in?"

Contemplating my next move, I look back at Antwon. "Wait. We'll see what they want, then let them have our hearts and souls!"

"I'll let the others know!"

Red

Antwon quickly makes his way to the others. Looking at the ship, I see it beginning to make its way into the cove. A fire burns red on her deck and rowboats are being lowered into the water. We wait as five of them head towards shore and the men on our ship ready the cannons. Finally, the men on the rowboats wave as they come ashore. I see an English uniform and begin running towards him, wanting to know how they know we are here. The man turns and my breath is taken away from me.

"Jack? What are you doing here…what's with the uniform?" I ask, shocked by this betrayal.

"Hi Jane. Yes, it is quite a surprise to me as well. I will tell you over some ale."

"Of course, come. You look ridiculous in that." I answer. "Sit. Why have you come here? Especially wearing such clothing?" I ask, confused, looking him over and over again.

"I bear news from England. According to what they heard, from my mouth, they believe a certain Red witch, as they put it, is dead. I have received two thousand pieces of gold from both the Spanish and the English."

I gasp, at a loss for words. "Are you crazy? What do you think they are going to do when they find I am not dead? They are going to kill you!" I reply, angry.

"You let me worry about that, but now you can get well without them hunting the seas for you."

I shake my head, "you don't understand, Jack. You probably lead them right to us. That bounty was for me, not for what was maybe me. They probably knew you were a friend or just wanted the gold. Either way, we must get ready to move. Get ready to move out!" I shout to my men.

"No, Jane. They gave me a commission and everything. They really believe you are dead."

"Jack, listen to me. Please," I say, grabbing his arm. "They only gave you that so they could hang you for treason. After all, you now serve the king. You also abide by their laws. They most likely sent ships out after you left. I know the English, and I know the Spanish, too. How do you think I am in the spot I am? I trusted them and they used me. Now I am fighting to live every day while they fight to kill me. You meant well Jack, but you should go before they catch you here and hang you."

"I will not leave your side if that is the case."

"Go. Before I have your death on my head to. Please save your life, and your wife and kids, too. Forget you know me. Just forget about me until we meet again after this life," I shout, grabbing him and forcing him to walk to his rowboats.

"Jane… ships are approaching," Antwon shouts.

"Go! Before it is too late. Get ready to board our ship; we must get moving. Go, Jack…NOW!"

Red

I watch Jack run to the rowboat as we begin to load ours. By the time we are done, Jack's boat has disappeared into the distance. We haul up the anchor and begin pushing out into the open sea. After a while sailing west, the distinct sound of cannons rings. I grab the spyglass and look for smoke. I spot smoke coming from four different places.

"Damn it. Damn them to hell!" I shout, lowering the spyglass. *"I knew it. The English followed him."*

"What is it, Red?" Regal asks.

"I think they are attacking Jack."

"Should we go help him?"

"There is no use. There are at least three, maybe four, ships firing. It's a lost cause. He was dead even before he left Death Island," I reply, tears falling from my eyes.

"Why did he come here anyway?"

"He made a deal with the devil. He told them he killed me and got the rewards offered by both kings. He thought they would lay off of us. He didn't realize that was for my body, not his word," I reply, taking a deep breath.

The cannon fire stops and I look through the glass again. Smoke is the only thing visible. I lower my head, tears seeping down. Everyone walks away, leaving me alone with my sorrow. I cannot help but feel anger. For what the English did, but also for what Jack did. I remember Jack and I running around, so carefree. There were only ten years between us. We picked flowers in the fields overlooking the vast oceans, talking about how one day we would be the greatest explorers of our time."

Red

An English Man's Revenge

Three days after the passing of Jack, we battled two English ships. We took their gold and burned their ships. After stowing the treasure on Death Island, we find ourselves yet again ready for a fight. In the distance, there's another ship bearing a Spanish flag. Our sails full and our cannons loaded, we head towards them. I have a hunger to watch them perish beneath the waves. A gnawing feeling eat away at me the closer we get.

"What's wrong, Red?" Regal asks.

"I don't know, but something about this ship is not right. Let's turn around." I answer, the feeling getting worse.

"Turn around!" Regal shouts to the crew.

"Why are we turning away?" Christian asks, confused.

"Something is off with that ship. Look at the way it's built. It looks like a reinforced warship; we wouldn't stand a chance."

"I see what you mean. She is a slave ship, Red. Look, they are pulling the oars out," Regal replies.

"I bet they are turning around. Hurry, let's set sail quick. Fire the cannons and slow her down a bit," I shout, watching the ship coming at us.

The cannons blast away, and I watch as oars are smashed into pieces. Once we finally turn fully, four English ships are ready to engage us coming around two small Islands.

"What are we going to do?" Antwon asks.

"Let me think. We could fight, but four against one is hardly odds favorable in the best of times. I think it is time for me to pay for England and Spain's shame. I want you to take the men and get off the ship. They want me, after all. I do not want you all dying for me. I will pay for this alone. You all have been the greatest crew a woman could have, but this I must do alone."

"Red…" Regal starts.

"No," I cut him off. "Please, just go and save yourselves. One day we will be together again. Now go before they are in sight."

I watch them all disembark as I lower the sails, giving them time to get to the island under the cover of our ship. Once I see they are close, I raise the white flag slowly. With every pull, it makes me want to vomit. Finally, it sits high. The English ship hits mine. I hear laughing as a man walks to the edge of the deck.

"Well, what do we have here?" Mr. Hawkins asks, snidely. "The one that scoffed at the notion of ever being part of the king's navy. Perhaps you should have taken my offer. I guess that ship has passed. Where is your crew?"

"I am alone. I was on my way to gather them," I answer, hatred filling my heart with every beat.

He glances towards the shoreline before replying. "You're lying. Even you cannot fire a whole row of cannons by yourself in that short of time. No matter. I will send soldiers onto that Island and I am sure they will be dead by the time the sun rises tomorrow. Now, you are a prisoner of England. Soon you will be part of a much greater fleet. Hand over your sword."

Looking at him standing on the deck of his ship smugly, I want to thrust my blade deep into his beating heart. I refrain and hand my sword to him, handle first. He reaches over the side and grabs it quickly.

"I see barnacles have your tongue. You are not as snide as you were at our last meeting. I have hoped you would be joining my ship. Now, please come with me." Turning to his crew, he adds: "take her to the gallows and make sure she is at the oar alone. I have a special treat for the vigorous woman whose tongue is open to lashing others."

"Yes, sir. This way, wench," an Englishman shouts as he grabs my arm.

He pushes me towards the English ship, but my eyes fixate on Mr. Hawkins, with fire in my soul. Feeling swords poking me in my back, we walk down into a dank smelling piss hole filled with men chained to oars. Some cheer from, and the whip master lashes them. Walking past them, we finally reach a lone oar. The man pushes me down and clamps a chain on my neck.

"This is her majesty's crown ship, and she has never had a person escape. You will enjoy your stay here. Oops, I mean I will enjoy your stay here," the whip master addresses me.

I stare at the English man with hate in my eyes as they chain my hands to the oar. They grab my foot and clasp an ankle bracelet on as I kick at them. When they are satisfied, I'm not going anywhere, they stand back and Mr. Hawkins slinks his way over.

"I see that you are no longer tongue lashing me. Soon we will be back home in England, and the king will distribute your body parts between his majesties flagships. But not before making you pay dearly for each of the English men you have murdered. I will enjoy watching your pain at his hands."

"Your king is the murderer, Captain. He falsified those documents. He did not want peace with Spain, he wanted Spain to start a war with him! I just happened to be the one there to blame," I shout, feeling the stinging lash on my back.

"Silence that tongue," Hawkins yells back. "I do not care what happened previously. I have been guaranteed a commission to command my own fleet under him. All I have to do is capture you. Thanks to you I will enjoy commanding ten ships and I will ensure pirates like you will never destroy another English ship again."

"Do you really think my death will stop other pirates? You're madder than I thought. My death will not stop anything," I reply, thinking.

"Oh, my dear Red Dead Jane. It's not your death the king wants, it's your pain. You see, he knows you set those ships on fire with the men still aboard to burn to death or drown. The king wants you to suffer the way they suffered. Only when you can no longer beg for death will he kill you and place your body parts on each ship. He promised me I could place your head at the bow of my ship. You shall provide me the good fortunes you had in the past."

"I will curse this or any ship the English have before brining any good fortune to any of you!" I answer, feeling the whip lash my back again.

Red's Pain

I have lost count of how many days I've been chained to this oar. Richard will feel my steel before I die, that I promise. I receive thirty-four lashes a day for the ships I sunk. I look at the other men chained to the oars and every once in a while, one looks at me expectantly. I do not know what they expect me to do.

"Listen up, sea scum," Mr. Hawkins yells, walking down the stairs. We will be in England's port soon, and you will have the luxury of spending one more night here. At first dawn you will move to the dungeons to answer for your crimes against the crown. Some of you will find the king lenient; others will find the punishment quite harsh. That all depends on what you did…right, Red?"

"Grab a cannonball and jump off the ship," I answer.

"Knowing what is going to happen to you, I would think you would have kinder words. Twenty lashes for everyone. You can thank Red for this." He places is hands behind his back and walks out.

Red

As the lashes begin, I hear the whips snap against our backs, meeting our bare skin and leaving their distinctive marks. After they finish, I lay looking at the bloodied backs of the others, only imagining what my own looks like. Sick of this shit, I try to pull the chain again, and everyone looks at me. I look towards the deck and a shadow approaches the hole but backs away again. I pull harder this time, trying to get the spike to come out, but it's caught in the wood too well. I spend most of the night trying, but to no avail. The sunlight creeps through the oar holes.

"Time to get up, pigs! You have your day in court," the whip master shouts.

We shuffle about, and my back is killing me. They bang out the spikes, but standing up is next to impossible. When men fall, they are beaten until they get up. I stay standing and after a few moments water is thrown on us. After sitting in our own filth for God knows how long, this feels good. They push us out onto the deck and the sun burns my eyes like nothing I have ever felt before. As we are marched off the ship onto land, people gather around. When I walk by, there are cheers as the English people throw their garbage at us, hitting me with some. Finally, we get to the stockades and they place me in the first one closest to the stable where they have the horse's shit. The flies and smell are awful.

"Ah, Red Dead Jane," Richard says cheerfully, coming towards me. "I see they gave you the deluxe accommodations. They're well suited for the likes of you. I am going to ask the king if I can have you sentenced to my ship instead of you wasting away in these dungeons. After all, I still owe you plenty for damaging my ship. I will make you pay it off, Red. You will be my personal slave and you will like me. I make sure everyone knows their place on my ship, and that includes women who think they are better than men!"

Glaring up at him, a smile comes over my face. "I will get my pleasure as well, when I plunge a dagger in your chest."

"I guess we will have to lash that unladylike behavior out of you."

"Do your worst, I will still cut you down," I answer, smiling.

"Yes, I am sure if I gave you the chance you would. My dear Red, I would never let you near anything sharp. We will see what King James says before we get too far ahead of ourselves."

"I know a few things that you can do with your king since you seem to enjoy being close to him."

"You must be looking to enrage a king. That's not something I would suggest personally, but you are welcome to ensure his fury if you must. As much as I have enjoyed this titillating chat, I must go. Enjoy your trial, Red. I sure wish I could be there to see what happens, but I am just as sure you will be able to tell me all about it when you are aboard my ship."

"Go rot on a pile of stinking English men."

"Tsk tsk. Etiquette my dear. Etiquette."

Red

Watching as he walks off whistling, I ponder: *"I will kill you, Richard. That is a promise I intend to keep."*

Looking out at the courtyard, I see them constructing gallows for the impending trials no doubt. I am sure the English judges will be righteous in their duties.

As the day passes along, afternoon turns to evening and guards patrol by. Cannons fire as another ship comes to port. Laying at the back of the cage, I grab a sack to use as a blanket.

"Hey, wench!" A man shouts. "Get up! Hey, Wench!"

I open my eyes to see four English guards standing outside the cage.

"Finally awake I see. I would not want to see you late for your trial. Get up!" One of the men addresses me.

Standing up, I wonder if I could grab his sword away from him and kill him before the others killed me. I walk by him as the others hold their swords towards me. He grabs the chain hanging from my neck, bringing me to a halt.

"Now that's a good little wench. I guess you are not as tough when your ship is not beneath you."

"One way or another, I will make you meet your maker," I answer.

"I will yearn for that day, but I fear you will have prior engagements. Now, let's go before you are late."

We walk through the yard past the gallows into a building. Three men sit at a table wearing red robes. The guards place me in the center of this room, pulling down on the chain and fastening it to the floor where I am kneeling. More people, including the king, walk in and are seated. After everyone sits, A man walks in front of me and states loud and clear:

"Your majesty, thank you for joining us today. It's our privilege to have you here."

King James stands and replies, "thank you! You may proceed."

"On this day, the 23rd of September of 1622 A.D., it is charged that Jane O'Malley, better known as Red Dead Jane, is hereby charged for treason to the crown of England. This charge stems from October 16 of 1620 A.D. for replacing Royal documents to incite war against Spain, causing King Philip of Spain to declare war on us. Treason carries a sentence of death by hanging, but King James would like to see her placed on a flagship where she will sit until she is dead, chained to an oar for the remainder of her life."

"Does the accused wish to say anything before we bring our sentence down?" the man in the middle asks me.

"Yes, yes I do. Your king hired my ship to carry these messages to King Philip of Spain in August of 1620, which I did. I never looked at any of these messages, I just delivered them. In October of 1620, I passed the message forward as I did every time before. I brought the message for King James back to England and two days later I hear I am a traitor to England. So, I left never to return."

"I would like to say a few words about these lies," King James says, standing. "Yes, this is true. We had an arrangement for the Lady of the Damned to carry these messages to King Philip. I was in awe when I learned that this wench stabbed her own king in the back, causing war to persist…"

I turn to glare at him as I interrupt, "lies! Nothing more than lies!"

The judge slams something down as he screams, "silence! You had your turn to speak."

"I was cut off by the king. You never let me finish having my say!"

"We have heard enough to know exactly what you did. We are ready to pass the sentence down. Jane O'Malley, you will hereby be sentenced to serve your time on the Flagship Prince Royal for as long as you live. Consider yourself lucky you are not hanging in the courtyard."

As they undo the chain from the floor, I stand up still shouting. "You will pay for this. All of you will pay." I see fear in a few of their faces, but others laugh.

"Get her out of here. Her voice fouls these four walls," the judge orders.

Walking hesitantly out of the building, they pull me along and back to my cage. They push me in, slamming the door shut.

"You're lucky. If that was me, you would be hanging. Tomorrow is your lucky day, Prince Royal comes in," the guard says.

"Drop dead!"

"I think you will first," he laughs. "That ship goes through scum like you quick!"

The pair laugh as they walk away. A man comes by later in the day to drop off a bowl of something that was supposed to be food. It looks like vomit and smells like it too. I'm in the middle of dumping it outside the cage when a little boy walks by. He stops and looks at the food on the ground before grabbing a piece of meat and eating it while walking away. Watching him eat almost makes me sick. Before he is out of my sight, he stops walking and falls to the ground, shaking erratically. People come running to his aide and a man grabs the boy, lifting him up and running past my cage.

I sit here in silence, looking towards the sea until a man walking by interrupts my thoughts.

"Jane…?" he stops in front of me. "What the hell are you doing here?"

"Timothy?" I ask, looking closer. "What are you doing here?"

"I'm gathering supplies for the winter to come."

"Ah, yes. I'm here because they've sentenced me to the Prince Royal for treason. Lies, but that is what the king is about."

"I know they are lies. I remember a friend saying you were set up by both ends."

"Hey, you! Move along!" A guard shouts, coming up behind Timothy.

"I better get going. Good luck Jane," Timothy says, turning to go quickly.

"Yes, stay safe," I whisper.

He slips away as the guard comes closer, looking to make sure he did not leave food or anything else behind.

"Looks like your friends will soon be hanging," the guard says, leaning against my cage. "Guess you can see the gallows pretty good from here. Makes you wonder who are the lucky ones. They will hang for a day, but you will die on that ship."

"What makes you so sure I will die on that ship?" I ask, glaring at him.

"We have named her the executioner! There are only three men that have ever made more than one voyage. Any woman who has boarded has never made it back. I am sure that is why the king sentenced you to her. What I would give to be there when you realize how bad she is…"

"You are all the same. I will get out of here, trust me."

"I will watch for you. It looks like they are ready to begin hanging. I'll make sure the view is clear for you to see. Enjoy," he says, walking towards the gallows.

He will be my first kill when I get out of here. I can only look as man after man is marched up to the top and walked over to the noose. They stand tall, not one weeping, knowing this will be their end. Each one begins their descent into deaths waiting arms, flailing before slowing to a swing. For the rest of the day I watch the breeze give them life.

Shortly after the sun makes its way down and the stars begin to twinkle, the serene moment is disturbed by a huge amount of cannon fire lightening up the port. I stand, trying to get a view of what it is, but cannot see.

"Well, I guess your luck just ran out. It seems the Prince Royal has arrived early," a soldier tells me, coming closer.

"You mean that is the ship?" I reply, stunned by the number of guns.

"Yes. She is indestructible and undefeated. As I said, she has taken more lives than you have. Captain Munroe, better known as Captain Death, is of the strictest attitude. Even his own family fears him."

"It makes no difference, I will still come back for you all."

"I will be waiting. Enjoy your sleep, Red. You are going to need it."

The Prince Royal

Laying under the ratty looking sack, I try to keep from freezing to death from the chilly night air. A well-decorated man walks towards my cage and stops a short distance away, gazing down at me with distaste as the torch lights flicker across his face. He shakes his head ominously as a soldier hands him a piece of paper. He glances at the soldier with a slight nod and then turns back towards me.

"This is the traitorous wench?" he asks. "I should just hang her from the highest mast of my ship now and do away with this scourge of England. We'd be better off for it. Just look at that red hair. Why King James would have hired her in the first place is beyond me."

"Yes, indeed, but you would enrage King James," the soldier replies. "He seems to want her death to be gruesome and as lasting as long as possible, Mr. Munroe, sir."

His eyes fall towards me again and then back to the gallows in the courtyard. Taking a deep breathe, he replies aptly annoyed: "very well. For the king. But I will not tolerate anything that comes from her forked tongue."

The second man nods, "Fair enough. The king cannot fault you if she speaks. Just wait until you are at sea before doing anything. Just in case King James comes aboard and wants to see."

"Alright, Dickens. You might as well wake the wench up, they've already put the others on."

"Yes, Captain Munroe. I will get her aboard immediately."

The captain nods happily, placing his hands behind his back as he slowly walks away. Stopping, he turns around one last time.

"Tell the men I will be ready to leave at six bells."

"Aye aye, Captain. Six bells."

When the captain turns, the soldier unlocks my cage.

"Get up, Red. Your ride is ready," he yells angrily,

He grabs my chain and pulls me out of the cage, almost making me fall on my face. Three more soldiers come to aid him as I pull back on the chain just as forceful. One of them grabs my hair and the others grab my arm. After a brief scuffle and a couple of head butts, they manage to keep me under control.

"Tis your lucky day indeed," one of them grumbles. "Any other day and I'd have gutted you for this. Let's get her on board before I do something the King will punish me for later."

They drag me towards the massive ship and I can't stop thinking about how I am going to get out of here? Surrounded by hundreds of English soldiers, we walk up the gangplank. We head down the walkway to the lower decks where the oars sit and there are over a hundred men chained to the oars. A man stands at the back with a drum in front of him.

They sit me down and take the neck chain off, replacing them with ankle chains on. They slam a spike into the beam on the floor, attaching us all to our seats, before disappearing up the stairs.

A short time later, heavier footsteps and a shadow appear, followed by a man dressed in red. A cold, deathly look is in his eyes as he scans over each one of us.

"Well, well, well. I see we have quite a few people here. This ship is his Majesties Flagship Prince Royal. Since she has been afloat, this ship has been undefeated by all enemies of the crown. Any thoughts of escaping should be placed out of your heads. My men will shoot you if you even twitch the wrong way. You will get one meal a day and if you don't like it, I don't care. You will have a ration of water and once you are done that's it until the sun rises again. You will sleep at your oars because you are aboard this ship to serve out your sentences. If the man next to you dies, we will remove them at our leisure. Rest assured, you will die eventually. If you speak, you will get ten lashes. If you do not row, you will receive lashes until you row again. Are there any questions?"

I watch as Captain Munroe comes down the aisle.

Red

"Yes…" a man at the front begins.

"I said no speaking, swine!" a crewman yells out.

The man with the whip walks by me quickly, headed for the front. He hits the man rapidly. Another crewman takes his whip and begins to lash a man a few rows back. The snaps of the whips are disheartening, as are the men's screams of pain. The Captain smiles, satisfied.

"That is twenty lashes. I said no speaking; you all are to be quiet. Let this man's stupidity be a lesson for the rest of you. Every time one of you does something, the man four rows behind will receive the same."

Looking at the smug look on his face, I stare at him with detest in my eyes. He catches my gaze and makes his way towards me. Hands behind his back, the captain leans into my ear and whispers.

"What is your problem, wench? Do you object to the way I run my ship? Well? You cannot speak now. Did you really believe that a whole navy would fall beneath your feet?"

Wanting to speak, but knowing what will happen, I just look at him and imagine plunging my sword into his mouth and down his throat. A smile must have crept over my face, because he backhands me.

"If you ever smile my way again, I will pull you apart in the pulleys of the sails, wench!"

He abruptly turns and walks back to the deck. Everyone looks at me. The little smirks and nods of approval replenish my hopes to get out of here alive.

After what seems like hours, a small cannon fires. I hear the words 'one hour' and a man comes down the lane, counting us as he walks by. Once he counts us, he and the other men leave.

"You're Red Dead Jane," the man next to me whispers. "Do you remember me? I tried to join your crew. John, John Welligham?"

"Yes, I remember you…"

"I must apologize for the way I acted then. I understand now what you said back then, that your ship needs blood. I became a member of another ship within hours after you left. The ship was sunk by the English two hours after we left. The Captain jumped ship as the battle started and I could not see why he would do something like that. That is when what you said sunk in. If your crew holds the ship in the dearest regards, and the Captain holds the crew to those same ideals, then everyone will protect each other."

"Shh, someone is coming…" I whisper, hearing footsteps. A shadow comes towards the opening, and a man looks down at us before turning and walking away. "Yes, that is why we were the way we were. We always fought for the ship and each other. Everything else is just a thing you can do."

Red

"I see that now."

"I have been sitting in a cage, waiting for this ship. They told me my crimes were best suited for this ship."

"Was your crew hanged yesterday?"

"No, I told them to abandon the ship and head to safety," I reply, trying to keep it quiet. "Why? I thought to fight to the death was an honor?"

"Have you ever heard of living to fight another day? I sacrificed myself so they could continue fighting on," I answer.

"You are one hell of a Captain, Red."

Glancing at the shadow above, I place my finger over my mouth and he nods. Soon, a burly man walks down the ramp and stops at every row to check the chains. Placing my head down on the oar, I watch him out of the corner of my eye. He continues until he reaches the last row, and I have to turn my head slightly so I can watch him. He finally sits down at the drum and places his head down. Soon he begins to snore, and I look over at John who is also sleeping. He is a shell of his former self, and half the weight he was when I last saw him.

I'm startled awake by the boom of six cannons firing. Sitting up and looking around, the sun is peeking through the oar slots.

"Sit up straight, the captain is coming," the burly man shouts, stretching.

A few defy the order and are swiftly whipped until they're sitting straight. Captain Munroe comes down the walkway, his hands behind him. Stopping after the third row, he looks around at everyone.

"You're a bunch of pathetic dogs, the lot of you. You are property of the Price Royal, and as such you will do as you are told! Any deviating from his majesty's orders and you will find a new order of horrors. I will not hesitate to make examples of each of you, and I assure you, you will die in a most diabolical manner. Mr. Hanson, you may sound the drum at one quarter reverse until we reach open seas."

"Yes, sir. Lower the oars, you dogs!" the drummer commands.

Lowering the oars, we try to find the rhythm and begin pushing and pulling according to the drum beat. A cannon fires as we start rowing forward, and the first mate comes down to inspect the rowing motions.

"You! Get in step with the others," he shouts, pointing at the row in front of me.

He pulls his whip and cracks them swiftly, almost hitting me as he swings wildly. Eventually they get the motions right, and he walks away.

"Next time you'll receive twice as many," he calls back.

Red

The Seventh Day

Seven days on this ship seems like seven years. Two men have died and their bodies remain at the oars. They passed away three days ago and the smell is as awful as anyone can imagine. One can only hope they remove them soon. It's been non-stop rowing with barely a few hours of sleep in between as the Captain wants to make the next port within a few days. While the drummer sleeps, Angelo, the man who sits in front of me, and I discuss what we could possibly use as a way out of this hell. The one man we have to worry about is the drummer. Since we left port, he is the only one to not leave out of our sights. If our plan can go off without a hitch, we should be out of here in a week's time. Only these next few days will tell.

"Psst…Red?" Angelo leans backwards toward me.

"Yes?" I whisper, listening as someone walks past the opening.

"The sounds coming from the deck above. It sounds like they are preparing the cannons for firing. They are either going to port or they are getting ready for a battle."

"Yes, probably a port. They have not begun a faster drum beat. I wonder where they're taking us this time." I ask confused.

"I do not know, but I am sure we will find out soon enough."

Before I can respond, a shadow appears at the top of the deck and a man walks down to stand in front of us all. I have never seen this man here before. Another man, the Captain's first mate, follows him down. They walk down the aisle, looking at us each as they pass, talking amongst themselves. They point at different people as they continue, marking things down. They stop beside me, and the man stares towards me intensely.

"Is this who I think it is?" he asks.

The first mate continues to write, replying unconcerned, "This is Red Dead Jane, if that's who you're thinking of…?"

"Oh yes, yes indeed. Red Dead Jane, I have been wanting you for many months. I was so pleased to learn of your ship's sinking. I want her for my ship. She will be worth her weight in gold."

The first mate glares at me, his eyes filled with hate, as he answers reluctantly, "yes, she is quite a prize indeed. She is also the king's prize. I do not think you will have this one Mr…"

Red

"I must have her!" the stranger interrupts. "I owe her so much for what she did. I want to show her the same kindness she showed my father's men. She deserves everything I have to give her."

I do not remember seeing this man when I attacked ships. I wonder who he is? Why does he talk like this? Was he a man who jumped overboard, or was he wounded?

"I will ask the Captain, but it is unlikely you will get her," the first mate finally responds.

"I must have her. This kind of swine needs to learn! I lost so many people to her and her band of dogs. Please inform the Captain that I will pay triple for her and I will also take those two, there and there. If I do not get her, I will not buy those two either!"

"I will ask the Captain, follow me."

"Who was that?" Angelo whispers once they've left. "That man is enraged with you. What did you do to him? What are they up to Red? Are they putting us on a different boat?"

"I don't know who he is. I don't recall ever seeing him before. I was told all but three men ever returned from this voyage, and I think I know why now. Most men do not die. I believe this Captain sells them to other ships. I bet his king does not know that he is profiteering." I whisper.

There is the sound of footsteps fast approaching and the Captain, followed by the first mate, the stranger, and other men come down, stopping in front of me. Captain Munroe scowls.

"Are you sure this is the one you want? She is not worth one gold piece, needless the twelve you are willing to pay. I would feel as if I were taking advantage of your generous nature…"

The stranger holds his hands up angrily, and shouts, "Captain Munroe, I assure you. To me, she is worth every gold piece. I would be revered back home for bringing such a disgraceful sea hag to our doors. I have been waiting for so long to get my hands on her, so I am willing to pay this price for her. I assure you Captain, what you would do to her is nothing compared to what I have planned for her. When I'm finished with her, she'll be as red as that hair of hers!"

"I wish I could be there myself to watch this scourge bleed. That being said, I am not one to argue with such a distinguished man as yourself over such as her. I will let you have her, and I will even throw in that man right here as a gracious gesture."

"Many thanks, Captain. I am sure we will have such business dealings in the future as I regain my fleet."

"I look forward to many more endeavors. Come, let us have a drink and finalize the details while my men place them securely onto your ship."

The pair walks away while the others come down. They bang out the spikes and pull each chosen man out of their seat. When they get to me, they place a neck chain on me again. Once they remove all the leg shackles, they pull me out of my seat and I hit the floor with a thud. One shouts and kicks me in the ribs.

"Get up, wench!"

Red

They whip me until I get up on my own and then they chain us together, marching us out onto the top deck. The fresh air is crisp and the clouds are moving along quickly; a storm is coming. Walking across the plank to the other ship, we are taken down to the cages where they place the three men in one cage. They walk me to the far end where the animals are kept and throw me in with the pigs.

Sitting here in the filth of these animals, I wonder what's next. Our plan was flawless if everything worked in our favor, but now I must find a way out on my own. I stare at the cargo, trying to figure out where we're headed now.

A man walks to the cage, and stops to look at me.

"Excuse me. Who owns this ship?" I ask quietly.

"I'm not supposed to talk to you," he answers, looking around cautiously. "The captain will be down here as soon as he finishes up on the Prince Royal."

"Can you just tell me where we are?" I ask.

"I'm sorry, but I must be going now."

Before I can say anything else, he scurries away quickly.

I turn back to my companions and see the pigs are staring at me. "What are you looking at?" I shout.

What a Mess

Hours after being put in this cage, it feels as if we are finally beginning to sail. I wonder what more I can endure before I have had enough. The pigs snorting and squealing is beginning to agitate my last nerve, but darkness finally arrives.

A lantern comes my way and stops in front of the cage. The man who bought me holds the lantern to his face. stands there holding the lantern to his face.

"Hello Red. Do not worry, I am a friend."

"I don't even know you. Who are you anyway?" I ask.

Red

"My name is Jameson. Many months ago, my father Edger Townsend was boarded by pirates. This pirate went by the name of Red Dead Jane. Instead of taking anything, this pirate gave him food and a few supplies to get home. My father, who was barely alive when he arrived home, said that the English merchants sold them rotting food. Everyone was either sick or dead. When you came along, you were the angel they needed. You saved my father. Before succumbing to his ailment, he said if I were to find you in trouble of any kind, I was to repay you. Captain Munroe has been selling people for years off his ship. When I saw that fiery red hair, I knew right then who you were. You made my father happy and helped him home so I will help you get home. I know where Captain Munroe said you were captured, and we are not but three days away. Would you like to be dropped off there?"

I smile as I remember that old man. "Yes, I know that Island well. I will be able to get back home from there."

"Let's get you out of there and cleaned up," he replies, opening the cage and helping me out. "I am sorry I had to put you in here. I told them I would treat you as a pig. I do apologize for anything I may have said out of line. The English play hard when it comes to these kinds of dealings unless they figure the person is going to get worse than what they are giving."

"Believe me, I know. That is why when I have my ship and crew back, I will hunt them to the ends of this world."

"Your ship was sunk. They destroyed it shortly after taking you."

"I guess that's one more thing the English will have to pay for," I answer, lowering my head as we walk.

"Yes, I know you will get your revenge for what they have done. Come this way."

He leads the way to the upper deck and to a room where three women are waiting.

"These women will help you clean up, and then we will have some supper. I will be back in a while, Ms. Jane," he explains before exiting the room.

The three women begin taking off my tattered clothing and tend to the wounds on my back. After four baths, I finally feel like I am part of civilization again. They brush my hair, and clean under my nails.

"Your hair is so red and beautiful," the lady brushing me says. "It feels like silk. I am so very envious, Red. May I inquire to where you got the name Red Dead, Jane?"

"Red was originally given by my father and mother for how intensely red my hair looked. Dead my crew gave to me. After I was branded a traitor by the kings of England and Spain, my crew noticed that on the onset of every battle, the cannon fire was directed to where I was standing. Even when we boarded their ships, they always went for me first. I would not be alive if it weren't for my crew. You can guess Jane, so I will not bother with that one," I answer as she continues to brush my hair.

"That is amazing," another lady responds. "You are an inspiration to women like us."

"What? Are you not free women?" I ask, confused.

"Oh, we are very free," she quickly answers. "But just knowing there is another woman out there, doing as you do, gives us hope that one day we will see more women in charge of ships such as yours."

"One day all women will come together and fight for what is right," I answer, smiling.

"That will be a pleasant day, Red."

A knock on the door interrupts us, and one of the ladies has a brief conversation with whoever is outside.

"Yes, we will bring her there shortly," she says, closing the door again and turning back to us. "Dinner will be ready in ten minutes."

They quickly dress me as they continue to chatter about my hair. Once they finish, they stand back and grin.

"You are gorgeous, Red. Shall we go show you off?"

"Yes, I'm starving." I answer.

We head to the main hall where Jameson stands waiting.

"No lovelier woman has graced this room. Please, have a seat."

Curates

After three days of hellish conditions, the sea finally suspends the tormenting winds. The waves were as high as the deck herself, but only one man fell to what I presume was a quick death. Four others suffered serious injuries, one of whom will probably not survive. He keeps bleeding slowly from his mouth and is not moving well. I hope they will all recover from these wounds as they have all made me feel welcomed. Not one man, woman, or child has tried to disrespect my lifestyle. They ask many questions about what I do, and even a few would like to join me. We had to change my docking plans as the English have occupied the original island. I am sure they are searching for my men.

"Well, Red, I guess this is where we part ways. Thank you again for everything you did for my father," Jameson says.

"Yes, he was a good man. I am grateful as well. Maybe one day we will meet again in a time where there will be peace at sea and no more fighting to survive one more day."

"I would enjoy that, Red," he replies softly. "We have some food and other essential supplies to keep you going for some time."

"Thank you, Jameson. I will not forget what you have done for me." I answer.

"We will not forget you either, Red. May the seas provide you plenty of great victories."

"I believe the seas shall be on both our sides Jameson," I say, placing my hand on his, as a smile emerges on his face.

"Yes, I believe these seas will."

Making my way into the rowboat, a woman hands me a musket. I descend to the waters below and we head towards the island. With every stroke the ship shrinks in the distance, and the land nears.

Once we hit land, we unload the boat, and Franklin adresses me, "it has been an honor to hear your stories, Red. Perhaps we will meet again."

"I have enjoyed the stories of your family as well. We will meet again, in this lifetime or the next," I reply as he shakes my hand before getting into the boat.

"Take care my friend!"

They row back to the ship as I begin moving up the beach into the trees. As the sun beats down on me, I find a shady spot and put the sack down. Picking through the items, I only take the lighter items I can carry. Hours go by wandering through the humidity, swatting away flies and all the other insects.

I hear what sounds like Spanish voices coming down the road, so I lie down in the swampy terrain until I see the Spanish conquistadors. There are thirty of them marching along.

"All clear, sir," one of them shouts.

After they pass, I wait to see if any others come by. When no one does, I stand up and make my way to the road. I'm walking quickly in the opposite direction when gunfire breaks out. I turn around, pistol in hand, as the gunfire intensifies. I change my direction and move towards the noise. When I get there, I see the entire Conquistador squad lying dead. A familiar looking man is leaning over one of them.

"Regal? Is that you?" I ask.

He turns towards me and grins as he shouts excitedly, "Red? You are a sight for sore eyes. Guys! Red's back!"

I watch as most of my men come wandering out of the heavy bushes, cheering.

"Where the hell have those English bastards been holding you?" Antwon asks.

"Where do you think? England of course," I reply, happy to see them all.

"Of course. I am surprised they did not hang you," Christian answers.

"That would be too good for me. They threw me on a ship, the Prince Royal. When we get a ship, we will have to watch for her. She is loaded with cannons. Luckily for me, the Captain sells the people held there. An old friend purchased me and dropped me off on this Island."

"Well, I am glad you are back," Regal says, giving me a hug. "Between the English and the Spanish, we have been fighting nearly every day. One of the dying Spaniards happened to say they were on their way back to their ship. We were thinking of capturing it."

"Well, we need a ship so I say let's check it out."

We change into the conquistador's uniforms and continue along the road until we see a ship docked in the port. Hiding in the bushes, we wait and watch to see what they are doing.

We wait until it's dark before to make our move. Twelve of my men sneak up to the ship's supplies sitting near the gangplank. Two conquistadors stand guard at the bottom, so we march towards them.

"Stop! Who goes there?" one of them calls out.

They both look towards the trees, pulling their muskets up and taking aiming. Before they can say anything, our men run out from behind the crates and stabbing them from behind. We drag them to the edge of the dock and throw them into the water.

A couple more conquistadors make their way to the gangplank, holding lanterns to see what the noise was. They walk down the plank, and as soon as they are down at the bottom, they're both stabbed and thrown into the water. With no one else coming, we make our way onto the ship.

Looking around cautiously, I see another guard. Holding my sword tight, I tap my foot against the wall.

"Who's there?" the guard whispers.

I tap my foot again, and this time his footsteps make their way over. Just as he turns the corner, my sword thrusts into his stomach. Christen quickly grabs him so I can pull my sword back.

We continue to make our way, taking out guard after guard as we look for the Captain's quarters.

"You go to the guard's chambers. The rest of us are going to release the prisoners," I tell Regal.

"Okay, Red. Meet you back here in a while," he whispers before leaving.

We continue to kill as we go down to the lower deck where everyone is sleeping. I make my way to the drummer and can't help thinking of the drummer on the Prince Royal.

Standing behind him, he wakes up in time to see my sword meet his heart through his back. He flops over crashing on top of his drum with a thud, stirring the prisoners.

"Shh!" I whisper, as we start pulling the spikes out, releasing them.

Making our way back up, we meet Regal. We stand outside the Captains' quarters and fling open the door. The Captain's face falls flat seeing us standing here. He angrily begins pulling his sword, but before he can do anything he's grabbed and held by four freed prisoners. His sword drops to the floor.

"What is your name?" I ask, walking closer.

"That is none of your business, wench!"

"You tell us now, or you will be our prisoner on the lower deck."

"Let's go then. I have nothing to say to the likes of you."

"Well, gather any of the other men," I say to my group. "We will show them what it is like to be chained to these oars."

When we get to the oar room, the prisoners chain the crew to the oars. Once finished, I try again.

"What is your name, Captain?" I ask, aggressively.

"When the king hears of this outrageous act, you will hang on his personal flagship!"

"We are going to have to take that fire from your tongue, Captain. Whip them! We will set sail shortly," I instruct the men. "Who here can work cannons? We will teach these Spanish how we get people to talk. As for you lot," I say, turning to the freed prisoners. "After we reach our destination, you will be free men. You will be welcome to either join us or leave."

They begin to whip the captain and his men as we return to the upper decks.

Shortly after we pull away from port, we see a lantern waving back and forth from another ship in the distance.

"Load the cannons on the port side. We will signal them back when we get close enough." I say.

"Aye, Captain!" Antwon responds grinning,

Within a few minutes, we catch a breeze and start moving faster as we approach the other ship. They are still waving the lantern when we send the first round of cannon fire into their lower decks. We set off our second round just as they send their first. Their shots hit the lower decks with the prisoners. Our second shots must have hit below the water line as the ship starts to lean on her port side.

"Keep those cannons loaded, we still have a ways to go," I shout loudly.

"We've lost five of those Spanish prisoners, including the Captain," a man tells me, coming up from below deck.

Red

"Too bad, I was looking forward to making him suffer," I answer.

"Red, there's another ship on our starboard and she's coming in fast!" Regal shouts.

"Do we know which ship?" I ask.

"No, but it looks English."

"Okay, fire when able. We are not worrying about gold. Let us just defeat them and make our way to freedom!" I shout.

Everyone runs to different stations, as the ship comes within range. They fire first, putting a hole in our sail and splintering the wood. We return fire. We fire back and forth, unsure what damage we are causing them, or taking ourselves. After a while, the cannon fire seems to be coming from three different ships, and they're ripping our ship apart at the seams. "Everyone, get to the rowboats!" I yell. A man comes running up and states.

"Why? We can take them on. We have the man power to overwhelm them," a man tells me.

"I do not know who you are, but we are outgunned three to one. Get to the rowboats and maybe we can get on one of those ships while they are busy firing at this one. Go!" I shout, angrily.

Watching everyone lowering the boats, another round of cannon fire sounds. There's screaming and a rowboat crashes into the water.

"Get them down! They're firing at the boats," I yell, pushing a man aside. The rest of the boats hit the water quickly, and I slide down a rope into a boat below.

We row towards the ship on our port side. The cannon fire subsides as one ship approaches what is left of the Spanish Galleon. We finally reach the ship and use the ropes to climb up the side quietly, getting to the top. We take the crew out one by one until we are in control of the ship. Armed with a new ship, we stop to consider strategy.

"Let's take this ship out, the other one is blocked by that Spanish Galleon we were just on. When you are able, fire. I will turn the ship enough for you to hit it," I say, pointing to the ship closest to us.

"I'm on it," Christian replies, smiling.

We turn slowly until finally our cannons light up as they smash into the other ship. A fire starts to burn as we raise the sails. We unleash another set of cannon fire. It does little damage, but she is still on fire.

We continue to sail the way we were originally headed, leaving the ruined ship as we slip away into the dark of night. Encountering no more surprises, the crew and freed prisoners meet on deck.

"I am Red Dead Jane, and you will sail with us until we reach our destination," I address the freed men. "You will all be free men after that," I say to a round of cheers.

"Where exactly are we heading?" one of them asks.

"I do not know yet as that depends on who is following us in the morning," I answer, looking into the darkness. *"Who knows what tomorrow will bring."*

Freedom

A week on this ship and we finally have land in sight; a much better sight than what we saw a few days ago. We took on two English Galleons and sunk them both within hours of each other. Other than being slower than the Lady of the Damned, she has held up pretty good. Some of these men are good because they have been on warships before. I can tell by their manners. As we approach an Island near Spain, I say goodbye to twenty-seven men. Watching as they slowly paddle towards the shore, Regal interrupts me.

"Damn. They were some of the best right there. Where to now, Red?"

We continue to watch the rowboats shrink in the distance as I turn towards Regal. "I know this may not be what anyone wants to hear, but I am thinking of going to confront King Philip of Spain," I say.

A few seconds pass before he replies: "You're right, Red, that is not what I wanted to hear. You will be hung upon landing on the shore. He will make sure of that."

Red

"I know, but we cannot keep battling both sides like this. There are only seventeen of us left. Even if we resupply, the English and Spanish are not alone anymore. They have gotten wise to our tactics. How long will it be before we are in an unwinnable situation again? I have been aboard the English ships and they are far from pleasant. I do not want to end up on another one. I figure if we create a peace between us and Spain, then we may get their backing in the war with England. Look at that battle a week ago. Those ships were English and Spanish ships."

"At least send one of us in your place," Regal counters. "You are far too valuable for us to let you become captured again, or hung. Let me go, and if I don't come back you will know it wouldn't be safe."

"He does have a point, Red," Antwon says, nodding in agreement. "You are too important to die, especially at the hands of either of those madmen."

"I do not want to condemn anyone else for what I have done," I answer, looking around at their faces.

"Yes, you have honor and take your responsibilities seriously," Christen says, stepping forward. "This time you should stay back and let one of us repay your last deed. There's no need for you to go through that horrific ordeal again."

"I see what you are saying, but I do not want to choose which one of you to go."

"We can go into the details ourselves," Regal says, putting a hand on my shoulder.

"Okay. I wish whoever it is the luck to come back. I guess we'd better set sail for Spain's shores."

I walk over to the railing, and stare out into the open ocean before continuing to my cabin, closing the door behind me. I walk over to the table and sit down. Pulling my dagger out of its sheath, I look at the blade shining in the light as my thoughts take over.

"I cannot let anyone sacrifice themselves for me. I am the Captain. And yet, I know I will surely die if I step foot on Spanish soil. Do I let one of them go on my behalf? They have served me well. I could not ask for better men…On the other hand, hanging is my future anyway. Every other pirate has been hung or killed. I must not let my respect drop into this uncertain vat of mindless emotions. Emotions are what will kill me in the end."

Goodbye, Old Friend

Three days of sailing later, it's seventeen of us against what could be as many as a hundred men as we come on the rear of an English flag flying ship. The ship looks vaguely familiar, but then again, they all look like this one.

"She has been in a battle," I say, looking through the spyglass. "Her port side looks in bad shape; perhaps we can take her down on that side."

"You're right, Red," Christen replies. "She has to be down half her guns. That would be an advantage for us. I am sure she is running to meet up with another English ship to escort her back home. I say let's do it!"

"What say you all?" I ask the crew. "Do we attack or leave her alone?"

"I say we do what we have done before. Let's get another notch in our belts," Henry yells.

"Alright, ready the guns and pull the sails up. Let us make her ours!" I shout, grinning.

I watch as everyone readies for another furious battle. As we come out of the gentle fog behind her, the ship tries swinging her starboard side to us, but she is too late. After firing four cannons off, someone aboard the ship raises a white flag.

As we come up beside her, all I see is a wounded man in a uniform that is tattered and bloody.

"Where is your crew?" I yell, feeling uneasy.

"We are but insufficient men who are mostly wounded…" the man shouts, holding onto the railing for support.

I call Erick over and whisper in his ear. "I do not trust him. I think they are going to try and ambush us. I want you to go and hit their working cannons. That way if they try anything, we will still hold the upper hand."

He nods and spreads the word to the others who begin loading muskets on the deck.

"What happened? Who is your Captain?" I ask, loudly.

"We were attacked by the Spanish. We sunk her but we lost quite a few men in the process. Captain Hawkins is dead…"

That is why this ship seems so damned familiar! I think. "Okay, we are coming aboard!" I answer.

Red

"This was the ship that took me to England," I tell Christen. "She holds a sea dog on her. Fire those cannons right away and take her out. I believe they have enough men waiting for us to board and they'll try to kill us if we do."

"Yes, Captain…right away."

Looking back at the wounded man on the other ship, I can see his eyes move towards the center hold, and nod to myself. Our cannons ring out, smashing into their hull, and the man looks horrified. I quickly drawn and aim my pistol, hitting him between the eyes. Red coats emerge like ants from a hill and my men fire their muskets, dropping them rather quickly.

"Shoot the red witch!" I hear Hawkins' voice ring out.

Another round of cannon fire obliterates their hull, but there is still gunfire from both ships for a good twenty minutes. I finally see Captain Hawkins emerge from his hiding place, hands raised and holding a sword. He looks at me with a distaste that I return with a smile, my pistol aiming right at him.

"Well, if it is not my old friend Mr. Hawkins. You English should really stay off the sea. It does not seem to be good for your health," I say.

"You wench. Why are you not dead on the Prince Royal?" he yells back.

"I am Red Dead Jane. I am the queen of these seas, and you thought a ship was going to kill me?" I answer, smugly.

Hopping over to his ship, I walk up to him and point my pistol in his face. He drops his sword and it clanks on the deck. He stares into the barrel as he responds.

"When the king said you were not going to be on my ship, I told King James he was making a huge mistake. How right I was. Had you been on my ship, you would be rotting at the bottom of the sea."

"I know you wanted me to suffer at your hands, but sadly it was not meant to be. I will enjoy my time with you, Captain. You see, I never really expected to meet up with you again. Sadly, it seems you will be the one dying here today!"

"Why don't you and I fight to the death?"

"I had thought about that, but you did not offer that same courtesy when I surrendered to you." I answer.

"That is because you were a traitor to the crown. You do not get the option of a death by sword."

Keeping my pistol on him, I lean over to pick his sword up. Still watching him closely, I jump back onto my ship.

"You can say I am a traitor, but I never betrayed anyone. Come on over, Captain. Or do you want to burn with your ship?"

"I will burn with my ship," he sneers, straightening his coat.

Red

Christen and Regal cross ships to tie Hawkins to the mast, and then proceed to loot the ship.

"You are a foolish captain. Most would not want that death."

"I am far from a fool, wench. I would rather burn in the infernal flames of hell than be known for being held by a treacherous wench such as yourself!"

"Oh, I see. I have another idea. One that will see you become the disgrace of England. I think it is quite fitting for you." I reply.

"Red, we have freed the prisoners," Christen interrupts. "They have agreed to join us. We have a lot of gold here, too. Spanish gold."

"I wonder if King Philip would like to know about that. What do you think, Captain?" I ask, watching him show fear.

"I will die right here, on my own ship!"

"Move the Captain to our ship. We will serve him the same hospitality he showed me when I was on his ship," I state, grinning.

Christen and Regal untie Mr. Hawkins and hold him at the edge of the railing. They carry him across ships, containing his flailing limbs until they disappear into the decks below.

"Where shall we sail?" Erick asks. "Our original route?"

"Thank you, Erick. I believe we should continue on our original heading. We'll take Mr. Hawkins to Spain where I am sure King Philip would be interested in knowing what England has been up to."

Staring at the open sea ahead of us, I'm interrupted by Christen coming up to the deck again.

"I have to ask, Red. What are your plans with him?" he asks.

"Oh, Christen. I have something very interesting in store for Mr. Hawkins. Very interesting indeed," I respond, placing my hand on his shoulder.

Red

A Fool's Day

Sitting here, in the Captain's quarters, I think of our upcoming days. We should arrive at the shores of Spain in the next day or two. Mr. Hawkins seems slightly disheartened by his quarters as a prisoner. Knowing how the English and Spanish conduct themselves towards prisoners, at least he will be able to tell others he understands what it feels like to be at the mercy of another's whims.

My plan seems to be intact as I have yet to inform my men that they no longer have to worry about who is going. I should tell them soon before the hour approaches.

Standing up and walking onto the deck, I look around and then up at the sky. It's a perfect shade of blue, as if the sea and the sky just make one continuous color with the sun highlighting the other. Bringing my eyes back to the task before me, I address the crew: "can I have your attention everyone?"

"What is going on?" Antwon asks.

"As some of you know, we were having discussions about who was going to talk to King Philip. I have decided we should all go and straighten this out. I cannot bear to not be part of whatever happens. I also could not live if something happened to any of you. I have an idea that I will run by you tonight during dinner."

I watch as they mumble between themselves, and walk back to my cabin. Closing the door, I sit down, unsure of what I'm doing.

I can see myself at the oar on the Prince Royal being whipped repeatedly, the pain of sweat and leather meeting. I cringe with every smack as captain Munroe stands nearby taunting me every few hours. He made sure I knew I would die in my own filth and that he would leave me there until that seat was needed once again.

"Red, wake up," a voice calls me out of the dream.

Opening my eyes, I see Henry standing in front of me.

"Huh? Oh, I must have fallen asleep. What time is it?" I ask, shaking off the sleep.

"Supper time…we're waiting on you."

"I will be right behind you," I answer, rubbing my hands across my face.

I walk to the galley where everyone is waiting for my announcement. When I finally get there, everyone stares in silence.

Red

"I can see everyone has been waiting for what I have to say. Well, I have decided I cannot allow any of you men to go into the king's chamber. I think it is best that we all go. I cannot let you go alone. We have an upper hand amongst us… Mr. Hawkins below. I believe when the King sees we have an Englishman, who sunk a Spanish galleon I might add, perhaps he will be more interested in what he has done than what we have done. I do not want to speak for any man here, so raise your hand if you are with me. Anyone who is not is welcome to stay aboard while we deal with this matter. If you do stay aboard the ship, make sure you are ready to sail."

"Excuse me, Captain Red? What would you say if the King of Spain were to vouch for your honor?" a man asks from the back.

"What do you mean King of Spain?" I ask, turning to face this man.

"I mean, I am the King of Spain. I heard your men talking about King Philip the IV. You see, I am King Philip; I was trying to find you, Red! We intercepted a message to King James from a loyal subject of mine two months ago. After we searched his quarters, we found my original dispatch to King James. Apparently, he and King James had an agreement; they bargained that England would win this war. I have pardoned you and your crew for crimes against Spain. Now, I need a favor from you. I want you to harass the English. I will give you three galleons to use under the flag of Spain. With three ships, you will never be the underdog again."

Confusion fills my mind as I stare at him. "Why? Why not tell us who you were instead of waiting?"

"Well, Red, for fear. I thought you would want me dead. Only when you said all this did I realized you did not want me dead. So, I took a chance and here we are."

"Okay. This man who switched the dispatches, is he English?" I ask.

"No, he is Spanish. He arranged to rule Spain once we were defeated. That is why we have encountered many more ships that are English; they are getting ready for an invasion of Spain. They have been trying to destroy my armada. I would not ask you, but the situation is getting out of hand."

"Fine. If my men agree, we will help you. What say you? Should we help the King?" I ask, looking around the room at the disgruntled faces.

Walking over to my men, we huddle close, "What do you all think?" I ask, looking at Regal's face.

"I do not think we should trust him, but I will go along if that is the decision."

"I agree," Antwon says, "but let's consider this as well. With three manned ships under our feet, we would need Red to pick two of us to lead on those ships."

"We could take the English on at their own game," I answer.

"Okay," Regal concedes. "I will agree, but I do not want a bunch of Spanish running around the ship. I say we pick the men who sail with us."

"Can we even trust them?" Christen asks, glancing over at the king. "After all, they believed you were a traitor before."

Fry, Die, and Drown…Living is not an Option

Fifteen days into our new alliance with the Spanish, we have drawn attention to ourselves from the English. They seem unpleased with our recent turn of events, especially with me being alive. They have upped the bounty on my head to ten thousand gold pieces. I do feel honored that they feel I am worth that, but this has brought out the pirate in everyone.

Four English ships are currently following us, and if our plan works, we should be fighting this battle on land. These English have a thing to learn about underestimating others. If all goes well, we will come across the Island and so will the English. Once we pass, our comrades on shore should hit the lower decks and sink each ship in the shallows. Forcing them to fight without their beloved cannons, the swamps will slow them down and the narrow paths will allow our numbers to even out. Today marks the beginning of the end for England. We will have them in such a state by the time we are done that they will stick close to home.

"Many pardons, Red," Christen announces himself. "We just received the signal from the island. They are ready and waiting for us to arrive."

Red

I grin, turning back to the English ships. "Great. Once we have them within our grasp, these four ships will be the start of their end."

"Yes. On land we can force them to go where we want them."

"They will stand no chance. Let's go see what is going on." I reply.

Walking out on the deck, I see the island fast approaching. I avoid the spyglass in case they are watching. As we begin to cross into the shallows of the sandbars, I listen to the bottom of our ship barely hitting the bottom as low tide starts. Once we manage to pass onto the other side, we turn to our starboard, drop anchor, and ready the cannons. No sooner had our anchor dropped than the English ships sailed into the channel.

The first ship comes to a grinding halt, as she begins to lean to her port side. The second one smashes into the first's stern and leans on her starboard side. The third one manages to swerve enough to miss the first two, but is stuck herself. The fourth one turns and that is when the cannons on shore hit her. The fourth is still floating, but disabled. We fire our cannons, hitting the first and third ships. We watch as the English disembark, heading towards the now unmanned cannons on shore.

"Ready the rowboats; let's join our brothers!" I shout.

As we reach shore and trudge into the jungle ourselves, we hear musket fire coming closer. We position ourselves so we can see who is running towards us. Four of our men come dancing through the vines. One drops after a musket fires, but the other three make it past us. Slowly, more figures emerge from the dense vines until we can make out a good twenty of them. We raise our muskets and pistols, aiming and firing. Some fall faster than the others do, but they all fall. Still hearing the muskets, we make our way towards the English ships. We reload and take aim at these ones.

"Kill them all! No prisoners!" an English captain commands. They fire at us as we scurry away back into the jungle. Making our way through the swamp, a couple of men fall to the poisonous serpents. We make it across finally, and wait for the English to follow while a few of our men come to join us from either side of the swamp. After waiting and waiting, we finally see movement coming towards us. We wait until they are in the middle before taking the first shots. Some fall because of our muskets, others are victims of the serpents that lurk in there. They begin advancing again so we retreat into the jungle once more. Slowly taking them down one by one, they have no chance to regroup.

Just as we make our way back to the shores, another contingent of English come our way, this time avoiding the swamp. Marching two by twos, we hide on either side of the path, ducking into the brush.

"Halt! Ready? Fire!" An English soldier shouts.

They fire at us wildly as they begin advancing again. Once they reach our positions we aim and fire, dropping them like flies. Pulling our swords and taking on the remaining ones, I run towards an officer. He aims as I swing my sword, cutting his hand and thrusting into his chest.

"Traitor!" he yells as he drops to the ground.

Once the last one falls, we start back to the shore again. We get close enough to see some of our men have been captured and are being boarded onto the fourth ship. We watch as they transfer their supplies from the other three ships to the fourth ship into the wee hours.

After hours of waiting, we make our way to the fourth ship and climb the ropes and their unguarded makeshift ramp. Killing the English one at a time, we finish what we started.

When we come to where they are holding our men, some are chained to oars while others are in cells. Freeing them all, we make our way to confront the captain himself.

I stop halfway up, noticing something's not quite right.

"Hey, this is a Spanish ship. What the hell is going on here?" I ask.

"The captains are still in their quarters," Erick informs us.

"Good, let's make sure there are no more surprises waiting for us before we confront these captains," I say, as we break up into groups and search the main deck.

There Are Too Many Captains Here!

After subduing the four captains and their first mates, it becomes abundantly apparent what is happening.

"Why Captain Valqua? Why?" I ask, confused.

"The King proclaimed your innocence, but I have not," he glares at me. "You killed my brother eight months ago and for that I will not forgive…"

"I will not apologize for anything I have done in the past. You can blame me for your brother's death all you want, but why are you not blaming the man who forced my hand? Why is that not where your anger is? Yes, perhaps I did kill him, but was he not trying to kill me?" I shout.

"Yes, but it was you who watched him take his last breath. You were there!"

"Maybe it was I, but anyone who tries to kill me or my men will feel death's grip. You are far worse than I, Captain. I became a pirate to survive, but you betrayed your own King for revenge. What do you think your king will do when he finds out? I agreed to help you, we all did."

"You are worth the punishment I will receive. Perhaps you would like to settle this out on deck?"

"Yes, as a matter of honor, I would!" I answer, grinning at him.

We walk out on the deck and he immediately begins thrusting his sword in hopes of piercing my heart, but I block every attempt. As he hastens his strikes, I pivot to the side and send him on the defensive. Taking high strikes, I make him leave his stomach area open. He hits my arm and a smile comes to his face.

"Take that, you wench!"

He takes a lunge and misses as my sword swipes across his stomach, tearing into his flesh. Before I can swing again, he has turned and is swinging madly. Sidestepping his forceful plunge, I quickly strike to his back, and my blade bites his flesh as he falls to the deck. Standing here above him, he shouts: "Kill me like you killed my brother, wench!"

"I will if I have to, but why do you not concede to this defeat and live to see another day?" I ask.

"I would rather spend my time suckling the Devil's teat than see you walk this earth for a moment longer."

"That is your choice…" I start to answer.

Before I can finish, he comes running at me with his sword headed straight for my heart. Dropping to my knees, my sword plunges deep into his stomach and out his back. I let go of my sword as he falls to the deck on his side.

"Red… I wish it were you… lying here…" he grunts.

Watching as he goes limp, I reach down and pull my sword out.

"Stupid man. I gave you a chance and now your parents have no one."

Turning my attention back to the matter at hand, we walk back to the Captain's cabin.

"Now, where were we? Ah, yes. You are now prisoners under the crown of Spain!" I state, smiling.

"How dare you," the English captain yells, slamming his fist onto the table. "You are a criminal yourself! You cannot place us as prisoners."

"That is where you are wrong. This letter of marquee guarantees my freedom," I respond, pulling the papers out.

He tries to come at me, but my sword raised to his throat makes him reconsider his options. He stops and backs up, moving behind his first mate.

"When King James hears of this, you are a dead woman."

"I have been dead since the moment your king put that bounty on my head, yet I still have breath in my chest. I am not in a box; I am standing here in front of you." I answer, smiling.

"You will be in a box, Red Dead Jane. King James will see to that!"

"I will be in a box when I am good and ready, and not a moment before. Your King will be long dead and I will still be on the sea, doing what I do best."

"You will never win, Red. You will always be beneath every English man alive."

"An English man does not come close to me without feeling the blade of their fate!" I answer, watching the anger grow on his face.

A King's Reward

We were paid five thousand gold pieces for destroying three English ships and bringing two Captains and three first mates back alive. According to King Philip, they will spend their time on slave ships. We have also received word from England that our deaths will bring someone ownership of Scotland. I guess the King is determined to give away what is not his to give. We board our ships, and get ready to sail to new lands, and hopefully our rewards.

"I will be in my cabin if you need anything," I tell Regal.

"Aye, Captain!"

Walking into my cabin, I watch the shores of Madrid disappearing in the distance. There's a knock at the door and Jasper peeks in, looking as if he has something weighing on him.

"Captain, would I be able to talk to you?" he asks nervously.

Red

"Yes, come in, Jasper," I reply, watching him sit down across from me with a distressed look on his face. "What is it you want to talk to me about?"

"Red, I am new to your ship, but I have heard great things about you. I must warn you of a plot to kill you. You know those three men that boarded back in Madrid? I heard them discussing ways to assassinate you in the tavern."

"Thank you for the warning. I must ask, though, what are you expecting in compensation?" I ask.

"I would like to join you. I mean, your crew. I am tired of moving from one ship to another."

"That's all you want? No gold? No treasure?"

"I do want that, too, but belonging to one ship is what I want most."

Just then, the door swings open and in walks a large man.

"How dare you barge in here?" I yell, but he continues.

The man pulls a dagger out and runs at me. I pull my pistol out and fire, hitting him in the throat. Jasper stands up and steps back as I kneel over the dead man. I'm pulling my dagger out when I see Jasper moving out of the corner of my eye. I throw my dagger, hitting him in the chest.

"Red? What happened?" Antwon shouts as he and Regal run into the room.

"Assassins paid by the King no doubt. I want those other men who came aboard off this ship right away."

"Yes, Red. They will be placed on a rowboat within minutes," Regal answers.

"Thank you. From now on, nobody else is to board our ship that we do not personally know. Regal, after you have made sure of their parting, we must talk."

"I will be back in moments," Regal says, leaving the cabin.

After he leaves, I saunter over to Jasper who lays with my blade in his chest. I grab his hand to see what he had planned to kill me with, and find a tobacco pipe. As I pick it up, it falls into two pieces revealing a little dagger.

"Oh, these tyrants are beginning to annoy me," I think to myself.

Walking out onto the deck, I address the crew members fueled by anger.

"You all work for the King; you want to kill me and collect your rewards. I have had it with these two trying to end my life. Why should I let you live another day? To let you have another chance to kill me or my men? I think it's about time we show the King of England what sending fools will get him."

Red

"To hell with the lot of them!" Christen yells as the other men cheer.

As they pull the men from the rowboats, there are screams as they're tied up one by one.

"I have been kind for far too long. I have endured the English ships- a hellish nightmare for those who have been prisoners on them, captains who are vile at the best of times, and a king whose insolence is a disgrace to the people and himself. I think we should show this proud King what sending people after us will get him!"

"What should we do to them, Red?" Erick asks.

"I say let's hang them from the masts so all English know!"

"Let's feed them to the sharks!" Henry suggests.

"Yes, let's feed the sharks. Let's see if they can taste the bitterness of your treachery. Put one man in a rowboat and let him sail to merry old England and tell the King what we will do to anyone else he sends our way!" I state.

"No, please Red," Michael pleads, dropping to his knees. "I swear on the bible I will never again attempt to come after you."

"More English lies. The moment you have a chance, you will come again. You will fail in your attempt, but you will come."

"No, I swear I will not ever come to your door again."

"You must take me for a fool since we have been on the seas. The only two things I trust are the ship beneath my feet, and the men whom I trust my life. You do not get that with the King! You think your King holds honor, but he does not! My men are more honorable. When one of us is in need, we are here together. You want to go back to your King? Fine, you will watch as your friend's take a daunting splash, then we will send you on your way to your King!"

I watch as these men squirm around trying to escape, as I walk over to the edge of the ship. I prick my finger with my dagger and watch as blood trickles down my finger and into the sea. I walk back towards the men and come to a stop. Another man stands in front of me, shaking. Looking at each of them, a smile comes over me that is big enough to have my eyes squinting.

"I know what you all must think of me, and I immensely regret what I have to do to you. You and your King have forced my hands to do this," I address the men. "I would never have considered this, but you all came aboard my ship in hopes of sending me to the depths of hell. I have let go of what most of England thinks about me, but coming into my home where you were welcomed? Disrespectful. I give respect to those that show kindness, but you have not. From now on, anyone who disrespects me or my men will feel death's embrace."

"Please, Red, I never tried to kill you!" a man yells.

"We will do this until the day the King of England repeals his order. The King of Spain admitted he was wrong and has made efforts to repay for his ignorance. Now, it is such a sorrowing event, but you must depart for your chosen destinations."

Red

I watch my crew put one man into the rowboat with a bottled message to the King. The other two are thrown overboard into the waters below and I hear the splash. Tied by a rope, they are dragged behind the ship, bobbing in and out of the water. After some time, we see fins emerging from the darkness of the waters, swerving in a zigzag motion coming closer to the two men. We lower the rowboat into the water and release it, and the shark fins continue to get closer. There's a burst of water and the shark breaks the surface, holding the man in his mouth and tearing him in two.

We turn away as the man's upper torso flies by like a rock out of a catapult. The other man disappears beneath the water as the rope stretches and then breaks. We bow our heads as a respect to the dead before throwing the other two in the water.

"England shall know, we will no longer tolerate these dirty tactics. If they want me or any other man on this ship, they will have to stand face to face and take their best shot! I will not be a spectacle in the King's games. If he wants my head, let him take it off my shoulders himself!" I shout towards the water.

A Journey's End

It has been a long time since land has been beneath my weary legs, and I can see on my men's faces that they are tired. Having set sail for Death Island, I did not tell them where we were headed. As I sit here in my cabin, the sky has the bluest sapphire tone I have seen in many months. The gentle motion of the sea cradles the boat as if it were her child. Standing up, I clasp my hands behind me and a smile creeps on my face. I know the serenity of this moment will forever be etched in my memories.

"What will I do with the treasures I have accumulated over this last year? Perhaps I will settle for an Island I can call my own, where only the truest of hearts will be welcomed. People who I will not have to wonder their motives or question their honesty. Yes, that is my dream after all this fighting is done."

The door opens, and Christen enters.

"Many pardons, Red. All the cannons have been cleaned and readied once again. The ship is at one hundred percent again. May I ask to rename the ship the Lady of the Damned II?"

I smile at the thought. "That is a great idea. Yes, you have permission to rename her."

I watch as he hurries out, and I hear him tell the others. I soon follow and make way to the deck where I see two ropes tied to either end of a plank. They lower Christen down with paint and a brush, and two hours later he emerges from the stern covered in white. He has the biggest smile as he announces the name change.

After all the celebrating is over, I head back to my cabin followed by Regal. He closes the door behind him and I sit down.

"Red, I know we have rode the winds for many months, and we have fought side by side even when we thought we were going to lose. I also know the people you left behind in the Americas. I am wondering if we should not set sails for those lands and visit the ones closest to our hearts?"

"Yes, we have been through so much together. So many fights against unimaginable odds, but here we sit, still breathing. Once we finish this last trip, we should head for home. So many people must think we are dead."

"Thank you, Red. I know you want to get this over with as soon as possible with the English and Spain."

"Yes, I look forward to not dealing with them any longer. I do not trust either king, and as soon as I have finished with them, I never want to see either of them as long as I live. I am sure they feel the same about us too."

"Yes, I am sure the feeling is mutual."

Time for Change

Ever since our arrival home, people have shunned us. Even our families seemed to forget us. Maybe the sea has changed us; made us more defiant to the rules of others. My mother was the only one who would let me in to visit. We talked about my stay on the English ship and the many ships we sunk. She reminded me of a time when I would not hurt a butterfly, or take the life of anything living. That is when I had to tell my mom a horrible truth.

I looked her in the eyes and said, "There comes a time in everyone's life when killing someone to save your life or another's is the only choice."

Her eyes teared up as she sat there. The more I explained, the less she wanted to hear, but I think she understood. I do feel bad, but I stand by my choices. As good or bad as they are, they are mine to own.

Walking around the yard brought back some of my most memorable moments. Playing by the pond and sitting in the moonlight with not a care in the world. I watched the light dance on the water, like when mom and dad would hold each other close. It's all but a distance memory. So many memories of times when everything was good. As everything must come to an end, so must this trip home. I feel the place we used to call home belongs to our former selves, and watching the others experience it is heartbreaking.

As we load the ship, I watch as people shun us, with only a few who think we are heroes for taking a stand. After we are loaded and ready to sail, my mom comes running as fast as she can, waving frantically. I run down the gangplank to my mom.

"Jane," she gasps. "I know this is hard for me, as it must be for you. You are everything to me, and I have never stopped worrying for one moment while you were gone. When those bounties came floating around here, I thought you had killed millions based on the size of the reward offered. I was so confused. When you came back, I was caught up in a whirlwind of emotions. I believed you did the worst things possible, but when you told me your side, I tried to understand how someone who loves life could do that. This morning, I remembered when you were ten. That raccoon was attacking your chickens, so you killed it!"

"Yes, I remember I kept hitting it until it died," I answer.

"Yes, you did Jane, so I do understand what you were saying the other day. You only did what you had to—to save someone else's life. I hope next time you make your way home, you do not have that bounty on your head."

"I promise there will be no bounty on my head. I love you." I reply.

"I love you, my dear Jane. Please write when you can. I know dad will get over his hate, and maybe he will understand what you are doing Jane."

"I will try at every port we hit; I know dad will get over it, he just needs the time to absorb what compelled me to do those things. I must get back mom, but I promise I will come back and we can do things the way we used to."

Giving mom a hug, I run up the gangplank with tears falling down my cheeks. The sails rise and we begin moving away from the shore. Mom becomes smaller until she is no more than a memory once again. Wiping the tears away, the land disappears entirely. Soon we find ourselves alone on the sea. As we sail along, a few hours go by before we hear cannon fire in the distance. We see smoke in the west, and I grab the spyglass to take a look. I see approximately twelve ships bombarding each other.

"Take a look, it is a good one," I shout, passing the glass to Christen.

"Holy. I can't make out the flags they are running, there's too much smoke."

He hands the glass back to me and I take a second look. Two of the ships collide while the others continue to fire on each other. The closer we get, the more carnage there is floating around us. Finally, coming up to the wreckage, there are rowboats in the water and bodies floating about being picked off by sharks. Screams for help ringing out all over. We throw a rope to one man in a rowboat and pull him up.

"What happened?" I ask, looking at his darkened clothing as he sits on the deck coughing.

"Thank you. We were ambushed by the Spanish and English."

"What do you mean by ambushed?" I ask, taken aback.

"We were part of a supply ship headed to the Americas. Out of the easterly heading, five ships appeared coming towards us, so we changed our heading to a westerly one, hoping we could evade them. Then we saw six ships headed for us from the west. Before we knew what was happening, they fired on us. We flew the white flag, but they continued to fire, sinking our ship, and then continuing on each other. We got into the rowboats, but with all that was going on, most were sunk by the falling debris."

Red

Red's Redemption

After weeks of sailing and trying to piece together what happened, the man we pulled from the sea, Johnathan Carve, was finally able to tell us the whole story. They were headed from the Americas to Asia to trade. They left the port hours before we did, and he is certain that both the English and the Spanish were firing at them. When I asked what the name of his ship was, he said "Gabriele", and that is when it struck me. The name of our ship before we changed it was "Gabriela." That told me right there that the English and Spanish were back together once again.

So, as we head to Death Island, we are entailed with a new boat we bought. We are going to fix her up and we will set the others afire. We are back to being true pirates once again, and I will never trust the word of the Spanish or English again. Today we will be free of any obligations to any country. Once we reach Death Island, we will begin plotting to devastate both countries.

Sitting in my room, I am again interrupted by knocking. I watch the door creep open, and Johnathan looks in, worried.

"Yes, Johnathan? What can I help you with?" I ask as he limps into my cabin.

"I know it is not my place to tell you what to do, Ms. Red…"

"But?"

"I was thinking…I know pirates are about the gold and everything else that comes with it, but you have helped more than you know. Can I ask why you do not stop? I am sure you have collected enough gold to buy more than your heart desires."

"Why is this any matter of yours?" I ask, annoyed.

"I heard before we left port that the English were rearming their ships. You know what they did to our ship, and that was within seconds. I feel like I should have your back."

"Thank you, but we have been through many battles. I am sure we can still accomplish our goals," I answer.

"Yes, I have no doubt about your abilities, I just do not want to see you lose. They have tripled the ship detail. You would not be fighting one ship, you would be fighting three."

"How exactly do you know this, Johnathan?"

"Please do not kill me, but I am English. I do not agree with what the king sentenced you to, nor do I agree with the bounty on your head. I am the first mate to the late Captain Emerson. He died during the sea battle. That is how I know, Red. I am sorry I did not speak up earlier, but I know you hate English with great intensity."

"Yes, I do," I say, pulling out my dagger. "But only because they keep sending people to kill me."

"That, I am not here to do. You saved my life, and I am forever in your debt. I will divulge to you everything I know about these ships, and I will not lie to you. They have heavier guns capable of smashing hulls, and they are now sailing in fleets of three or more depending on the cargo. When we were sailing, the Captain misread the ship and he ordered that ship sunk at all costs. The kings have a bet going: whoever sinks Red's ship would be rewarded for the deed. I know they are set to meet not far from here on Samana Island. I am sure they will be fortified on the Island."

Looking at the sincerity in his eyes, I release my dagger. "I thank you for your honesty, Johnathan. I guess it is possible to like one English man. Why would you tell me this?" I ask.

"You mean the Island?"

"Yes, that is puzzling me."

"I know you like challenges, and the Island is accessible from all sides."

"Yes, I know that Island. Why would they meet there?"

"That is the neutral place where they conduct their affairs."

"I see. Perhaps we should pay the kings a visit. I have an idea of how we can do it, too!"

"I will leave you alone then. Did you want me to send anyone in to take me to the gallows?"

I look at him, trying to figure out what he's playing at. "No, not yet. I want to consider this first. Thank you again, Johnathan."

I smile, watching him leave.

If he is correct, and these kings are meeting together, this will be the perfect time to kill them. If he is lying, though, it is I who will die!"

Twilight's Embrace

On this, the twenty-seventh year of my life, all four ships into what I refer to as the best worst day of my life. The three Spanish galleons separate from us to ambush the kings' ships while they have their little get together with a special guest who is not welcomed. I watch from the spyglass as the three ships engage the Spanish and English with cannon fire, leading them away from the port.

"When their ships leave, we will dock and I will confront them both," I tell Regal as he nods.

After an hour of waiting, the cannon fire can be barely heard and we sail towards the Island. Once are close enough, we lower two rowboats with a landing party.

"Ready our cannons!" I say quietly.

"Aye, Red," Antwon replies.

As the landing party makes their way towards the port, we wait and watch. The landing party attacks the soldiers by the dock and disembarks.

"Red, should we attack?" Christen asks.

I watch our men move a safe distance away from the ships before responding, "Yes! Fire when able!"

One of the ships returns fire, slamming our hull, but there is a second round of cannon fire from our cannons that she doesn't return fire. We wait, confused, for her to fire another round, but nothing comes. Dropping the anchor, make our way to land.

"I'll head towards the landing party and help them," Regal says.

"Yes, we'll head to their quarters!" I reply.

"Perfect, we'll cut them off!"

Jumping out of the boat and running to a nearby path, I head towards the guard's house. Finally, the first set of soldiers come running by with their muskets loaded. Pulling my sword, I swing at the first one that passes by. Watching as he falls, the others begin firing at me. Ducking behind a rock, the others with me return fire as I pull my pistol and join in. Once we take out most of them, Regal and the others join us.

"How's it going here?" Regal asks.

"Good, but there's still a few taking turns firing at us from up there," I reply, pointing halfway up the path.

"Go make the kings pay, we'll handle these ones."

Red

Four of us head towards the villas. Once there, we sneak up on a guard from behind and I stab him with my dagger. Making our way into the villa, I see the two kings sitting together like old friends through a window. Anger builds as I watch them laughing together.

Running across the courtyard, I take out various guards along the way. The other three men make their way along the path also taking guards out. Sneaking around the side, I slip into a door to a long corridor. Every step brings me closer to the kings that betrayed me. I slowly enter a room, hearing talking coming from behind two chairs. My sword pulled, I'm poised to strike as I step in front of them both.

"Red? What are you doing here?" King Philip asks, as both kings look at me with shock.

"You will pay for this! Guards!" King James shouts.

"Shut up!" I yell, holding my blade mere inches from his throat. "I am going to do the talking. I know what you both were planning, and I'm only glad you attacked the wrong ship. After I trusted you, Philip…why?"

"I am sorry, Red, but I too must be respected by my people. I was hoping you would not find the truth out. The people of Spain wanted you to pay for the people you killed. I really had no choice but to honor their grievances."

"I see, but as I have told many myself, if you hadn't deemed me a traitor, I would not have killed any of those people. You both left me no choice. You, King James, should be the one who pays for their deaths!" I shout, raising my sword.

"Do not put me in the same category as the likes of you! You had one simple order- deliver these to the King of Spain- which you did not!" he yells back.

"I did, but King Philip found your spy who changed his orders back to you!"

"Lies! Philip, you know I did no such thing…" he begins.

"Red is absolutely correct!" Philip interrupts him. "You see, James, I wanted to meet here to disclose to you a decree of war. I will act on it if you do not comply with my condition."

"What condition?"

"You must lift that bounty on Red's head, and pay her for her troubles, as I have. It's the only condition I have."

"You have got to be kidding me. You actually believe this pirate? Fine, Philip. For the greater good of the people. When I get back to England, I will tear up the bounty on this pirate's head!"

"No," Philip smiles, "I have papers here. You will sign them, freeing Red of any wrongdoing and agreeing to pay her five thousand gold pieces."

King James slams his hand on the chair and yells, "You are insane, Philip! I will not sign them."

Red

"Then I am sorry, Charles, but I must place you under arrest. My grievance with you is that you placed an illegal bounty on a citizen of Spain."

King James sits open mouthed for a moment, looking as if he is trying to compose a thought. Finally, he responds, "You have got to be kidding."

"No, I am serious. Red is a citizen of Spain, and as such she is entitled to her freedom. Now, you can sign, or a week from now you will have my entire armada at your port!"

"This is a disgraceful way for a king to act, or be treated. Fine, give me those papers."

I watch him sign and place his seal on them before throwing them at King Philip and shouting, "There! If you set foot on English soil you will be hung, Red!"

"I will not be there again for any reason, you befouled king!"

"Now Red, come let's take a walk. I will be back, James."

Outside, Philip hands me the papers.

"Red, I am sorry if I sounded harsh in there. What I said about the people wanting you to pay is true. Since you did time on that English ship, I waved your punishment. You are a citizen of Spain, but you are never to set foot on her soil again. I am giving you the one thing that has been taken from you, freedom. According to this order, you are free of any bounties. I will not say there will not be any people coming after you, but you are free."

"Can I ask you why you are doing this?" I ask.

"You remind me of a woman I used to know. She was much like you; always trying to succeed while others tried to trip her up. She died broken because no one would help her. I could not help her, but I am able to help you. I sent word to a great many people in hopes you might get word of this meeting. When I heard cannons firing, I knew you were here. I had ordered my men to let you pass, but knowing you, you probably killed some. You must know I respect you for your courage and honor, but after tonight I do not know you. You will move on to great things I suspect, and I will rule my kingdom while James rules his. Your heart is solid gold, do not let anyone take that away from you."

"I do not want to watch any more of my men die, and I am sickened by the things I have done. I let anger control me, but now I just want to be me. Now that I have my freedom, I have everything I have wanted since this whole thing began." I answer.

"You were a pirate to be reckoned with. My men told me stories of your daringness. I hope, after this night, we do not cross paths unless you are trading goods."

"After tonight, I do not think I will see you again." I answer.

Red

He grins as he holds his hand out, and I give him mine to shake.

"On that note, I will bid you ado. Live a long and fulfilling life, Red!"

He turns to walk back up the path, raising his hand giving a brief wave before disappearing around the corner.

"You alright Red?" my men ask, rejoining me.

"Better than ever. Let's get back to the ship. We will discuss this there."

A New Day Rises

Sitting at my desk, the Lady of the Damned II rocks back and forth in the current. My hands are cupped as thoughts of home dance through my mind. I glance at the papers that say I'm a free woman again, seeing King James' and King Philip's seals at the bottom of the page. As I stand up and walk out to the deck, I call the crew together.

"What's the matter, Red?" Regal asks, his face worried.

"I'll explain in a minute, Regal," I answer as everyone gathers around me.

"What's up, Red?" Christen asks.

"I am glad we are all here today. I know you all have been wondering what I've been doing this past week. Well, today we are finally all together and I have decided I am going to become a citizen of America again. I have been through hell with you all, but fate always has its plan for each of us. I have been feeling fate has been warning me that my time is coming soon, so I am hanging up my sword as of today. I know some of you have not been with us as long as others, but the last couple battles my heart has been elsewhere…

thousands of miles from here. I have received papers declaring our innocence, so we are free to live again. We have gotten the one thing no pirate has ever received – a pardon from two kings. I cannot stop any of you from continuing to fight the fight, but we have a chance to live as rich people. I will let you choose your fate. Thank you all for being by my side when times were good and bad."

"Red, it was an honor to serve under your command," Regal says, hugging me.

"Yes, you were the greatest Captain of all time!" Christen adds.

"Thank you all. It was truly my honor to have you all stand by my side."

As day turns to night, we celebrate, the night's auroras shine brightly in the northern skies. After everyone has fallen asleep, I begin taking everything I own off the Lady of the Damned II. By the time morning rolls up, I'm almost packed.

"What are you doing?" Antwon asks.

"I am taking my things off. This ship belongs to you who are staying with her," I answer, looking at the puzzled look on his face.

"No, this is your ship. It always has…"

"I cannot…"

"Put her stuff back on the ship," Christen tells the other men.

I watch as they haul everything back on while taking their stuff off, and placing it on the ground. After a few hours, everything is off.

"There you are, Red. She is yours, and may your journey bring you the happiness you want!"

"Thank you all. I will miss you and the adventures we have had together." I reply wiping my eyes.

We say our goodbyes as I board the ship followed by ten others who decided to come with me to America. We set sail, waving to those we leave behind. After sailing out of Dead Man's Cove, I finally go to the Captain's cabin. There is a note sitting on the table:

Dear Red,

Our many months together were the best of my life; you were always there when I needed you the most, and I hope I was there when you needed a friend. I have decided to continue with this life. I wish the best for you as our journeys take us in different directions. One day, we may cross paths again and I dearly hope your father has come around. I know the cost of everything you have been through and the stress you have endured. When you get home, depending on the season, I want you to pick the most beautiful flower and I want you to look at it closely. I want you to remember that you saw the world like no other; one filled with highs and lows. The flower you hold is everything beautiful that we all saw together. Each one of us carries that same memory. Your happiness is what you make of it, and beauty can be seen in everything you look at. Until we meet again, Captain Red Dead Jane.

Red

Christen Tambour.

Sitting here, smiling, tears stream down my face. As I look out the window and see the clouds making their way by, I'm comforted to know someone is thinking about me.

As the days turn into weeks, we finally reach the shores of home, and I expect the same reception I received the last time.

Heart's Home

Settling in at the port, I wait for the shouts and boos as I walk down the gangplank, but there are only cheers and congratulations. I nod as I pass the same people who just months earlier spit at me. I carry my sack as Antwon and Erick carry my chest of gold, and we finally reach my home. Placing it on the ground, we hug.

"Red, I know my words are just that, but I want you to know I am truly a better man for being on your ship. Thank you," Erick says.

They head down the road and disappear over the hill before I walk up to the doorstep of my parents' home. Stopping short, I stand there for a moment. Before I can open the door, Dad does it for me.

"Hello, Jane…" he states quietly, with a stern look on his face.

"Hi Dad, I…" I answer, looking at him standing there. A partial smile begins to emerge on his face. Just as I am about to apologize, dad quickly interrupts me.

"No, please let me. I know what you did was wrong, but I also know you only did what you had to. Weeks after you left, a man came to our door. He said he was looking for you and we told him you were gone. After he left, I realized he was here to kill you. I knew you were only doing what you had to do to survive. I am sorry, Jane."

"That is why I am home now. That is… if I am welcome?" I ask.

"You're always welcome home, Jane. Let's go talk by the pond."

"Okay, dad," I answer as he puts his arm around me.

We make our way to the pond and sit talking until the sun creeps down, creating an orange color in the water. That is when I truly realized I was home again. I can be that girl I used to be, only this time I have traveled to places only some wish they could. I feel so at ease here that I do not think I will ever leave again.

The End

Author acknowledgements

I would like to dedicate this story to Billy-Jean Marva MacKenzie, who became the face of Red Dead Jane. I hope, knowing you're not alone dealing with bullies, gives you extra strength to carry on being the girl you actually are. Follow your dreams, and they'll carry you far Billy-Jean Marva MacKenzie.

I would also like to thank my wife Teresa, who has endured so much dealing with me lol. I love you!

Thank you to Sam Stinn, for editing Red Dead Jane. Without you, Red would still be waiting in a folder for a few more years. Thank you!

Cover concept by Magen Baxman McMinimy. Thank you, I love the cover

Huge thanks to those who have followed me through this long journey, without you all, it just wouldn't be the same… thank you!

Red

Synopsis

Red Dead Jane, so named for her fiery red hair, is a pirate wanted by two kings. Betrayed by King James, Red is on a mission to clear her name of treason. Jane and her crew on the Lady of the Damned find themselves turning to piracy to survive, plundering every English and Spanish galleon they come across. Not to be deterred from her mission, Red battles the English and Spanish until she reclaims her freedom.